OTHER NOVELS BY MILDRED WALKER
AVAILABLE IN BISON BOOK EDITIONS

The Curlew's Cry
Fireweed
Light from Arcturus
Winter Wheat

THE

SOUTHWEST

CORNER

BY MILDRED WALKER

WITH ILLUSTRATIONS BY ROBERT HALLOCK

New Foreword by the Author

University of Nebraska Press
Lincoln and London

First Bison Book printing: 1995

⊗ The paper in this book meets the minimum requirements of American
· National Standard for Information Sciences—Permanence of Paper
for Printed Library Materials, ANSI z39.48-1984.

Library of Congress Cataloging-in-Publication Data
Walker, Mildred, 1905–
The southwest corner / by Mildred Walker, with illustrations by
Robert Hallock.—Bison book ed.
p.   cm.
"Bison."
ISBN 0-8032-9768-8
I. Title.
PS3545.A52486   1995
813'.52—dc20
94-40444   CIP

Reprinted by arrangement with Mildred Walker

THE SOUTHWEST CORNER

After that first meeting, I went across the road every day, and every day she called me "Honey Bug." And every day we walked up the hill behind her house. Each week she rode side-saddle twenty-four miles to a neighboring large town to tune organs in the large organ and piano factory there. On some Sunday mornings she would put a record on her Victrola. A few people drifted in and a few stayed outside. She played a song that was too sad.

> "I have you
> And you have me,
> Daddy"

It was sung in weeping tones by a tenor. Mother and Father would listen from our porch and I'd sit on the railing. People would get up, shake her hand, thank her, and leave.

When I returned to the village with my children for a visit after a number of years, I found my friend much older. She now lived in the southwest corner of her old house, and took her meals with her daughter's family, who occupied the main house. I remember that she gave me a small birthday gift.

Perhaps it was during this visit that my father pointed something out to me in a deed—the New England custom of having a southwest corner built for the parents to move into when a grown child with family took over the farmhouse. A few years later when I was between novels, I wrote *The Southwest Corner* as a long short story. My old friend from my childhood became Marcia Elder who didn't want to leave the hill farm she had been raised in.

The subjects of my novels were never formed in my mind when I began writing. Instead, the subject always started out from one small observation. For instance, one novel grew from my observation that winter wheat, a strain hardy enough to survive in Montana, was a combination of American and Russian seed. And, in the same way, the subject of a southwest corner intrigued me. My mother had spoken of her grandparents

living in a section of the farmhouse they had once built. She had to knock before going in for a visit.

Then, there was the story told in the village about my old friend, Mrs. Hamilton. She and her husband had left to settle in Michigan, but she had soon returned without him: during a severe lightning storm there a bolt had come through the roof, striking and killing Mr. Hamilton as he lay in bed by her side. I imagined how that might have been for Marcia Elder.

"Lightning won't strike me," Marcia says in *The Southwest Corner*. "I've given it plenty of chances since it killed my husband sixty-six years ago." That passage wrote itself very quickly—from the point of view of Bea Cannon's morbid curiosity. Some years after *The Southwest Corner* was published, I was told that a woman read it to Mrs. Hamilton in a retirement home, and she liked it.

When I first sent the manuscript to my publishers, Harcourt Brace and Company, an editor wrote back, "Honey, you can't write a novel about an eighty-three year old. Think again!"

In 1950, ten years later, I sent off the manuscript again. My husband, a cardiologist, was asked to give a paper in Paris and in Amsterdam, and I wanted to accompany him. I sent the manuscript first to my former English professor at the University of Michigan, Roy Cowden. He suggested firmly in his inimitable way, "Let us get seated." So I wrote the fictional passage that precedes the first chapter of the novel, describing the purpose of a southwest corner built into early New England farmhouses. I wrote it from the point of view of a visitor to an inn. It seemed a good way to "get seated."

This time Harcourt, Brace and Co. took the manuscript and gave it book-length treatment. Published in 1951, it was my ninth novel. It went on the best-seller list immediately even though I was told again by someone at Harcourt's, "Well, that eighty-three year old woman stops 'em." But the real story, in my mind, is that of Marcia and Bea.

In those days the occasion of a publication at Harcourt's was exciting. When my husband and I arrived in New York from

Montana, my editor, Bob Giroux, hurried in to take us to lunch. And when we boarded our ship for Europe, we found a basket of delicacies sent by the publishing house.

One comment made about my writing was that my things are good to put into a play or movie because there is so much exact pictorial detail. So I wasn't really surprised when John Cecil Holm inquired about writing a three-act play of *The Southwest Corner*. It opened in New York on February 3rd, 1955. I wasn't able to attend a performance because my husband was very ill, but I was kept informed of its progress by letters.

One of these letters, dated March 4, 1955, was from Eva Le-Gallienne. I was delighted when she agreed to star in the role of Marcia Elder, and after the play closed, she wrote me of her pleasure in acting the part. The following portion of her letter was in response to my letter thanking her for her role, regretting that the play had closed on Broadway after only a month:

"Of course I don't regret having played your wonderful Marcia Elder! I grew to love her very dearly—and was sad that more people could not have had the chance to meet her. I hope you would have liked what I did with her—or rather, what *she* did with *me*. I'm terribly sorry you missed seeing the play. It was, I suppose, too wholesome to survive in the Broadway Jungle—not 'sensational' enough."

Miss LeGallienne ended her four-page, handwritten letter expressing "sincere appreciation and gratitude for *your* Marcia Elder," distinguishing mine from the much changed Marcia Elder she had had to play in a TV version on the Kraft Television Hour. Of that she wrote: "I hope you didn't see it. I thought it ghastly beyond words—and I shudder to think of how awful *I* must have been! I loathe that medium—or rather, what 'they' do with it."

I was certain I wouldn't have liked the TV version, either. I had spoken on the phone with the two scriptwriters who believed that the plot needed the addition of a young couple. I

protested because I thought the story became trite with that addition. Further, the rewrite detracted from Marcia's own sense of delight in the hill farm, from her wonder—whatever her age—by giving those moments to the couple.

I too was saddened that the play, which had done so well earlier in the summer theater in Saratoga Springs, closed so soon on Broadway. One reason given was that it played simultaneously with Jessamyn West's *Friendly Persuasion*. Still, it was heartening to receive the following note from John Cecil Holm, written on the night of March 6th, 1955, when the play closed: "Mrs. Roosevelt saw a performance on Thursday night. She sent back word she thought it a fine and lovely play and that it was a reflection on the taste of American audiences that the play was closing. She thought it was a crime we had to close."

I find it anything but a crime, however, that the novel, *Southwest Corner*, is being reprinted. I hope it will "play" well for new readers. I was only in my thirties when I first wrote this novel, and now that I am in my eighties, I think Marcia Elder and I might be of like mind about many things.

Mildred Walker
September 1994

FOREWORD TO THE BISON BOOK EDITION

In the Vermont village where my family lived in the summers, I came to know Mrs. Hamilton, who lived across the road from us. One summer morning she came out of her house and called across to me:

> "Honey bug and molasses jug
> and sweet flagroot!"

The funny words hung in the air. I was four going on five. I started across the road but she called to me, "Honey Bug, stay right where you are till the oxen go by." A pair of oxen came up the road with their slow walk. I stood on the horse block in front of our house and waited. When she said, "Come!" I ran across the road. I didn't occur to me not to mind her. And so our friendship began.

"Il y a beaucoup de vieillards à quarante ans et une infinité de jeunes à soixante."

LAURENS

THE OLD three-story brick house on the hill looks like a Vermont homestead rather than an Inn well known for its bridle paths and winter sports. There is no place for the cars of tourists to stop in front and no tavern sign invites them to do so. A narrow path, bordered by phlox and tiger lilies, leads from the gate in the stone wall to the house. The white paneled door beneath the fan window swings wide enough for any Inn but the soapstone doorstep is too small for more than two people to stand on at the same time.

There is another door, set in the soft red brick, to the left of the parlor windows and partly obscured by a tangle of smoke bush and lilacs, that is identical with the main door except for its narrow width. It, too, has a fan above it, like a halo, an old iron doorpull, a large keyhole and heavy white wood panels. Beyond this door are two more windows, one of them cut off at the corner to fit under the roof, which slopes sharply down to the height of one story. This low sweep of the roof seems to make the brick house part of the hill that rises behind it.

I had stayed at the Inn two days and three nights before I began to wonder about the second door. On the warm July day it stood wide open, propped back with a conch shell, but none of the seven or eight guests at the Inn seemed to use it. I found no room that had such an outer door, and the only person whom I saw coming through it was the frail old woman who sat alone in the sun, as quiet as one of those gray backs of rock that crop out in Vermont pasture land, as much a part of the hillside as the firs and steeple bush and sweet fern.

I wondered what relation she was to the black-haired young woman who owned the Inn and went about dressed in jodhpurs and a jersey, who discussed wines or books or foreign cities with a knowledge that could not easily have been acquired in Vermont.

At length, I asked my Innkeeper about this second door and the little woman sitting in the sun.

"Oh," she answered, "that's Marcia Elder who sold me this house, all but the southwest corner."

I must have looked puzzled because she went on:

"The southwest corner was the way New England handled social security in the very early days. I had never heard of it until three years ago when Marcia Elder brought me to look at her home."

ONE

IT HAD BEEN the longest winter Marcia Elder remembered in all her eighty-three years. So many days of waking up to frosted windows and unbroken snow across the field, and the front path even with the meadow. Orville Greenstead came up every day or so, but he had tired of keeping the walks shoveled.

"Like I say, Mrs. Elder, you oughtn't to set foot out days like these as long as I can get up here or the Brady boy and, other'n that, there ain't nobody comes to see you so there ain't no real good reason for shoveling these walks way down to the gate."

"Except that I like the place to look lived in, Orville," she had told him. "That's why I don't close the upstairs

15

rooms any longer than I have to. You can let the paths go today while the snow's still coming down but by tomorrow I'll want them shoveled clean."

"Well, I s'pose you've got a right to your notions same as everybody else," Orville said. He pulled his ear muffs down as though to block out any more notions and went about the business of getting ready for the walk down the hill. He lived by himself just this side of the covered bridge and did odd jobs for Mrs. Elder in exchange for the wood he was cutting off the lower acre of her woodlot. As she told him, "You'll get the best of the bargain, Orville, unless I should live to be as old as Job." Marcia Elder didn't make a business of giving people the best of a bargain but this one made her feel free to see that Orville did what she wanted. The unshoveled walk bothered her. That was the way it would look some day when she was gone, but not yet. And then she forgot about Orville and remembered her brothers cleaning the walk and throwing snow at the window where she watched.

"Well, I'll see you tomorrow, then, Mrs. Elder," Orville said and opened the kitchen door.

"Better put another armful in the woodbox as you go out, Orville. It's getting down," she reminded him.

She liked a warm house even if keeping two fires going did make awful inroads on the woodpile in the shed. Orville grumbled about that, too, and the Brady boy who brought the paper to her and milk once a week said, "Mrs. Elder, you use as much wood as my Mother does cooking for all us kids. You'd oughter burn chunks in your sitting room stove."

"Maybe I should, Tom," she had said. She didn't think it necessary to tell him chunks were too much for her to lift. She was careful to bank her night fire with green sticks but it was a battle all winter and it tired her some. Most nights she went to bed about eight and it was hard to get up at twelve or so to put in fresh wood, but once she was up she enjoyed it. Sometimes she made a cup of tea at midnight with the little tea kettle on the parlor cooker or put a cup of milk to heat on top, and drank it standing by the stove in the friendly dark of the room. She didn't keep a stove going in her bedroom but if she hurried back the heat would still be in the folds of her challis gown and wrap deliciously around her legs. Then she could sleep till six when Tim, the tiger cat, jumped up on her window sill to be let in.

She didn't mind living alone; she had had enough practice at it. All these last thirty-two years since her brother died, but sometimes this winter she had looked so hard out the window and down towards the road it seemed as though she saw folks driving by . . . just for a second, of course. The road used to be so busy when the stagecoach passed by every day and oxen pulled the soapstone slabs down from the quarry, and children from the five farms up above went back and forth to school. Sometimes she thought she heard the creak of an ox wagon or the peddler's cart; the wind could make a sound like the tinkle of a peddler's bell. She had bought a little pearl-handled knife from a peddler's wagon once, so she could make a willow whistle with it, and her sister, Caroline, had told her that was nothing for a girl to buy. Caroline had bought a russet-leather sewing case. Now Marcia had them both.

She watched for spring this year more eagerly than the spring she was married, going out to stand in the sun before the snow was off the ground, before the sun was really warm, holding out her hand to feel it. It seemed so long since last summer when she had been warm all at once without bundling up.

The first of May came in warm, but she didn't trust it. The second week was warmer still. Monday, Tuesday, Wednesday . . . nobody could ask for a finer day. By ten o'clock in the morning the sky was bright and as warm as her blue wool afghan. Marcia opened the front door and the side door into the sitting room and propped the lattice door of the woodshed back with a stick so the air could stream through the house and drive out the close winter feeling. She let the sitting room fire go out and put only one stick in the kitchen stove and closed the dampers. By the end of the month, she told herself, she would move back into the upstairs bedroom where she could look out into the Maple tree and watch the little red leaves uncurl.

"Hurrah to Gideon!" Marcia said to the cat and felt as though her vocal cords were rusty from lack of use, so she said it again, louder. "It's time to get out of the house. If winter had lasted much longer I'd have turned into a mole." Marcia didn't talk to herself often but she sang sometimes, little snatches of songs like *The Battle Hymn of the Republic,* and *Oh, Dear, What Can the Matter Be, Johnny's so Long at the Fair,* or played the pianola, or read aloud to take it in better, both eyes and ears.

By noon Marcia had a packet of sandwiches, her thermos of tea, and her big old-fashioned blue wool cape, and was on her way up the pasture with her father's cane, that had a snake's head carved on the top.

There was a little snow yet on the north side of the stone wall, but wet and dirty-looking as though it were melting visibly. On the other side where the sun got to it, the new grass was bright green, each strong blade of it pushing up furiously towards the sky. She laid down her cape and the lunch things and plucked herself a spear of grass, drawing it through her fingers carefully so as not to cut herself. It could cut like a pocket knife, the edges were so sharp. She held it between her two thumbs with her knuckles tight together and blew on it, her cheeks puffed out like a chipmunk's. She made only a little squeak at first, but then she tried again, blowing so hard it took the breath away from her, but she did it this time, loud enough to set a squirrel scolding. Marcia laughed and remembered how she and her brothers and sister used to blow on a grass blade and Matt's shouting, "Marcia did it loudest!" She felt just as proud now, for an instant.

This was the first time she had seen the hill pasture since last fall. It looked so good: stony as ever, with outcroppings of wild rose bushes and last year's mullen stalks, that made regular Roman javelins when they were dry. The newly thawed ground was spongy under her feet, like a thick carpet after her thin rag rugs. She felt light-limbed and hardly stiff at all, as she climbed the hill to the cave of granite rocks they used to call the fort. The opening was under the pine trees and you had to crawl on your hands and knees to get through. You could stand upright inside but it always had a musty smell of animals that had wintered there. Once she and Matt had lighted a candle, but it was so damp and cold the flame guttered and they talked in whispers so long they frightened themselves. At Easter when she read the part about the women going to the sepulcher and finding the stone rolled away she always saw this fort, but with the opening made large so the sun could get in. It made her feel as though she had been one of those women on that first Easter morning and had seen the proof of the resurrection with her own eyes.

By the time Marcia came back to her cape the sun had gone beneath some clouds, and over to the southwest the sky had paled, but that was the way with a spring sky; it was like a sulky girl. In another minute, it would be bright again. She spread her cape against the stone wall and sat there to eat her lunch. Her legs had lost their light feeling and she was glad to sit down and drink the hot tea.

"Think of it, Marcia Elder, you have this whole hill to yourself!" she said aloud, but the sound of her voice embarrassed her. It was better to keep her thoughts to herself. She pulled the cape over her shoulders and head to catch a nap.

When she woke Marcia thought she was inside the cave. The cape had fallen over her face and shut out the light and she felt cold and damp. She started to crawl out and found she was not in the cave at all but sitting stupidly on the side hill. Wet snow was coming against her face and she could only see as far as the next mullen stalk.

She got stiffly to her feet, leaning hard on the snake-headed cane. Her cape trailed behind her on the wet ground and the thermos bottle slipped out of her cold hands and rolled out of sight down the hill. She should have known better than to lie down on the ground, she told herself. How could she have slept so long? The snow settled on the wide pink part in her hair and brushed her face. A little pain ran up her forehead from squinting into the snow. She sniffed and fumbled for her handkerchief and when she couldn't find it, she wiped her arm across her nose; she was too cold to care. She tried to hurry and tripped on her cape and kept her balance only with her cane.

There was little comfort in the house. She had left it wide open to the day and now it was as cold as a barn. Marcia pulled the lattice of the woodshed to and slammed the kitchen door behind her and hurried through the house to latch the front door. Both stoves were cold, she could tell by the color of the cast-iron.

She weaved a little crossing the kitchen floor and her hands shook as she took both of them to lift the lid off the stove. Somehow her wrists weakened and the iron lifter slipped out of the notch, letting the lid fall on her foot. She grabbed onto the front edge of the stove the pain was so sharp, and then, not meaning to, she sank down on the floor and clasped her hands around the pain in her ankle. A cold stove lid was nothing to make a fuss about; what if it had been red-hot? But it hurt.

The draught from the open window in her bedroom slid across the floor to where she sat but she couldn't get up courage to stand on her foot just yet. In front of her reared the wall of the stove with its implacable iron doors and she remembered when her head only came that high and she would put out one finger to trace the curlycues of the letters in the word *Imperial*. Her mother would snap her finger and say, "Burn! burn, Marcia!"

She must get the fire started before she caught her death of cold but she didn't move: just sat there and thought of all that had to be done to build a fire, as though by thinking about it she were doing it. The damper on the stove pipe was closed; it was a reach across the stove to turn it straight. The old papers were in the cupboard under the sink, the kindling basket was empty. The spring day must have gone to her head this morning for her to go off without filling the basket. The warm sunny morning was as far away and gone as her own thoughtless girlhood.

In her mind she crumpled the paper and laid the dry splinters of wood crisscross on top and scratched the match on the rim of the stove where the mark wouldn't show. Better to watch the flame take hold before you laid the first stick of birch on it. The loose edges of the birch-bark were quick to catch. She imagined the crackling sound so clearly she could almost hear it. Now two sticks of applewood and watch the color of the iron change. With the dampers open wide it wouldn't take long. She would sit here in front of it until the iron of the fire-box began to darken and then turn reddish.

Her leg cramped from sitting so long in one position

and she was shivering. Painfully she got to her knees and pulled herself up by the handle of the oven door. Her ankle throbbed when she put her whole weight on it. Maybe she wouldn't build a fire tonight; it was almost five. Just get on the couch and cover up.

Her cane was on the floor and it was too hard to bend again to get it. She made her way around the room from chair to table to dresser, through the doorway. The couch was just inside the next room. She didn't need any supper; the milk and eggs were down cellar, and the bread was way across the room in the crock . . . it was better for the old not to eat so much. She pulled the afghan on the foot of the couch up to her chin and doubled her hands in her neck to get them warm. She tried calling the cat. He could come in through the bedroom window and lie here on the couch with her to warm her up.

"Here, Tim. Here kitty, kitty, kitty!"

But she knew Tim's ways. When it started to snow he would go to the barn and curl up in a warm spot of his own after a meal of mice.

She was too cold to sleep. She lay watching the snow come against the window, not big flakes, thin grains of snow like sand. Already it was as dark as a winter's afternoon. The stillness bothered her. A cold house didn't seem friendly like a warm house did. Things seemed to stare at her: the spindle-backed rocker and the Seth Thomas clock and the high-boy, as though they resented her living on here so long, instead of Matt or Will or Caroline. The ticks of the clock didn't fall comfortably in the dark room; they stretched the minutes out too long.

What if she should fall and break her leg some time when it was really cold? Orville or the Brady boy didn't come by every day. She could freeze to death up here and nobody would know the difference. This was June and this storm wouldn't amount to much; it would get warmer right along now and soon it would be summer. But what about next winter? All those fires to build and keep.

She had always kept fires going, all her life, and never thought anything about it except to be thankful for a full woodshed. She was used to going out through the woodshed to the toilet in the barn; it wasn't like those outhouses people had down in New York state that stood right out in the open so you had to go outdoors to get to them. And there was nothing scarey about the barn. Even though the loft had been empty quite a few years, it still smelled sweet of hay. She always brought in a few sticks of wood and the cat's empty saucer when she came back so she saved herself too many trips. But now she began to think how cold it was going way out there, and what if she should be laid up. The ankle was a warning to her.

She dragged herself off the couch and limped painfully

out to the kitchen. You had to keep fires going or you were lost.

Orville Greenstead found her soaking her ankle by the kitchen stove when he came the next morning. She had such a cold she could hardly talk.

"You sure look peaked, Mrs. Elder, and sound worse," Orville told her. "It ain't right for a person your age to stay off up here alone. Like I say, you ought to have some woman here with you."

Marcia was strangely meek this morning. "Perhaps I should, Orville," she said slowly. There, her ankle felt better!

"Or move down to the village, maybe," Orville suggested, leaning his weight comfortably against the sink.

"No, I shouldn't care for that, Orville. I'm used to plenty of room and I've lived up here on the hill too long. Did you fix the latch on the barn door? The door banged last night."

But after Orville had gone she went on thinking about what he had said. She got herself so worked up she had to put on a warm sweater and go into the parlor to play the *Coronation March* on the pianola. Watching the keys move of themselves and the little marks on the white paper roll go round always pleased her. She sat on the high bench, pedaling with one foot and feeling that she was making the music. She had to stop to rest her leg but then she was ready to put in another roll. This time it was *The Battle Hymn of the Republic* and she sang with it so she didn't hear the Brady boy when he knocked. He had to come and stand in the doorway of the parlor before she saw him.

"Oh, Tom, I didn't hear you!" She hated to be startled.

"You was making too much noise, I guess. I brought yer eggs an' the paper. You didn't have no mail an' Ma sent a loaf of bread with the milk."

While she was thanking him she had a sudden uncomfortable sense of how she looked to him. Of what he told his mother about her: "Mrs. Elder was sitting all alone in the cold parlor playing music and singing to herself." The boy acted as though he wanted to run.

"Will you have a doughnut, Tom, or a cookie?" She wanted him to stay a little.

"No, thank you, Mrs. Elder. I gotta hurry." He was walking to the door, taking care to step from rug to rug. At the back door he stopped. "Oh, I meant to say, we're moving over to Stanton next month; I won't be bringing yer mail." He hesitated. "I hope it won't put you out too much."

"Well, I guess I'll have to manage some way, Tom," she said briskly. "But I'll miss you."

"Yes, ma'am." Then he was gone. She watched him walking his bicycle down the first pitch of the hill because it was so steep. When she came back from the win-

27

dow she wound the roll without playing the rest of it
and put it away in its box and closed the case of the
pianola.

June leaned a warm shoulder of sun against the kitchen
window and Marcia set Orville to putting on the
screens. From day to day, she watched the tiny leaves
on the elm trees grow full-sized, and as rough as a cat's
tongue, and the maple leaves spread out as big and
veined as the palm of her own hand. The hills turned
deep green, and by the end of the month there was
tender green lettuce in her garden to eat for supper,
with milk and sugar on it.

One afternoon in mid-June, Marcia put on her big
straw hat and went up to the pasture on the hill. Everything was there to see again, just as it had been in her
childhood. Queen Anne's lace, and steeple bush, and
yellow primroses. The yarrow was a coarse-looking
flower she and Caroline never picked but it had a good
earthy smell, and the little hard round yellow buttons
of the tansy blossoms were still fun to pull apart. She
went beyond the cave today and crossed the tumble-
down stone wall into the stand of timber to look for
Indian pipes growing in the roots of the trees. They
were waxy-white and turned black if you picked them.
"They're poison, and if you don't want to live, just put
them in your mouth and suck them; that's what the

Indians did when they were captured or hurt awful bad," Matt used to say. She had only half believed him then and she wondered now if he hadn't made that up. She picked one and held it in her fingers but she didn't put it to her lips.

Marcia was tired when she got back down the hill; she had gone farther than she had meant to, but a cup of tea and a good night's sleep would remedy that; a summer night with no fires to keep.

July was fine and hot. Noons the heat waves shimmered in the air and the grasshoppers fiddled away like good ones. "Loud as a factory!" Marcia exclaimed with satisfaction. She made a dozen trips a day from the house to the garden to water her flowers, and dug the plantain out of her front yard until she worked up a perspiration. It was so good to be hot.

Summer people came up the hill and picnicked in the orchard beyond the house and admired the great elms in the dooryard and looked at the date 1802 carved in the soapstone trim of the doorway. She didn't mind when they asked if she had any old furniture to sell or tried to buy the old settee out of her shed or wanted to know the names of flowers in her garden, but when they asked what she did all alone up here in winter, her voice grew a little tart. "Eat and sleep and breathe, same as you do," she told them. But every question like that added to the growing uneasiness in her own mind.

29

In August Orville drove her down to church and she looked at all the houses along the main street. There weren't so many as there used to be. She shook hands with folks who had white hair now whom she had taught in school. They acted as though she had lived in the time of Noah, except Asa Houghton who told her she had a better figure than these young girls. But she was glad to drive back up the hill. The village had a closed-in feeling. There were too many people living too close together. And she'd rather read her Bible than listen to that preacher going back and forth over one little idea, like a stocking darner.

August ran past the middle mark, but there were hot days yet to come. Marcia took her tea and bread and butter and applesauce outdoors to eat on the seat by the elm tree, whose green leaves were already mixed with a few gold ones. The swallows came swooping out of the barn loft just as they did every evening . . . but weren't they a mite earlier than yesterday? She didn't take the pleasure in them that she usually did. She sat idle with her empty teacup beside her and the applesauce hardly touched. Once her hand moved up to her hair to make sure she had taken out her kid curlers, but she had. She could feel the little white waves standing up on her head so they looked as though she had more hair. She felt the gold pin at her neck and fingered the little buttons down the front of her dress, then she joined her hands together in her lap as though the one could comfort the other.

"Well, Marcia Elder, what are you going to do?" She spoke aloud. Her chin looked more pointed when she pursed her lips. Her eyes that had once been a deep blue were as pale as the bluish cast of old windowpanes and showed the worry looking out of them as clear as windows. She had half a notion to wait till morning to make up her mind, but in the morning the sun would be warm and no sign of fall. It was better to think about it now with the air getting cooler all the time.

Well, then, she was eighty-three this summer. She might die any time. People did at this age. She wouldn't like to die off up here alone without anyone knowing. It would leave a shadow on the house where there had never been anything but life and sun and someone to care when a person died. Children coming up the hill for blackberries would run past the house and call it haunted.

She might get sick and unable to do for herself. The long and short of it was plain. She needed someone with her. If there were just some member of her family, someone she had a call on. With two brothers and a sister, a person would think . . . But Matt had died of consumption and Will had been killed in the Civil War and Caroline's only girl had died five years after her mother.

Marcia's eyes moved across the lawn to the second door

in the front of the brick house. Her grandfather had planned for his old age and that of his wife by building the one-story part onto the main house. It seemed so simple a solution: when his son married he deeded the farm to him, all but that southwest corner of the house. In her mind she opened the narrow door and went into those familiar rooms, three of them, and all as pleasant as anyone could ask for. She could remember as a child running in with a pot of beans from her mother's big oven, and listening to her grandfather tell about the days before Vermont was a state.

If things had turned out right, she should have had a son of her own to keep the farm and leave her the southwest corner. She sat a long time thinking how it might have been. But Life was pernickerty and didn't pay any attention to plans. She unclasped her hands and let them lie open in her lap. What couldn't be mended, couldn't, and there was no use crying about it. If she had no one of her own flesh and blood to stay with her, then she would have to get someone.

But she didn't have enough money to hire anybody. All she had now was this house off up here on the hill, and the furniture in it, and four hundred and ninety-one dollars in the bank. Her thoughts moved painfully along a path she had known was there although she had never wanted to follow it to the end before. The only thing to do was to make an arrangement with someone. Having come that far, she picked up her dishes and carried them in the house without looking back to see the last of the sunset or the swallows swooping in the dusk, or the elms against the sky.

She spent all week writing the advertisement for the Rutland *Times.*

> "WANTED: agreeable woman to share pleasant living with able-bodied, vigorous old lady of eighty-three with small capital, in return for all property at her death. Please give age and references when applying. Interview necessary."

She had hesitated over it and crossed out and re-written words and still she was dissatisfied with the final product. She didn't like the description of herself, but what else could she say? She was vigorous. She was able-bodied and eighty-three. Finally, she had put in the pleasant. "Pleasant living." That was what her life was up here; simple and pleasant.

The answers began to arrive sooner than she had expected. She could see that Orville Greenstead was bursting with curiosity when he brought the mail. He turned one letter over in his hand before giving it to her and asked if she had folks in Rhode Island. "None that I know of," she said without offering any more. Curiosity was worse in a man than in a woman, as bad as fussiness, she thought. Orville never did have too much on his mind, he had to fill it up with what he could.

She received eleven replies: four the first day, two the next, three that weekend, and two the next week. She couldn't bring herself to open them at once, and before each one she hoped that it would turn out to be from someone young; a young girl, full of life, not out of her twenties, someone pretty to look at, who would love to go up on the hill, and sing and play the piano and catch rain-water to wash her hair in . . . but that was foolishness. She knew that. Young girls didn't go off up on lonely hill farms to live with old ladies. They could get positions in the city.

As she read letter after letter, her hopes grew less. The authors didn't sound as though they had read the "pleasant living." They wrote that they had "had experience in taking care of the aged," that they "liked it quiet" and were strong and healthy. Several of the letters were written on coarse ruled paper, in careless handwriting by hands that must be red and heavy. Marcia had taught penmanship as a young woman. She could still write a hand that stood out on paper like a copper plate. With a kind of repugnance she laid aside ten of them. The eleventh, from a Mrs. Bea Cannon, age 55, was written in a firm hand on white paper. Its tone was capable. It stated frankly that the writer regretted leaving her own place in Dedham but did not have enough to live on without doing something. She presumed they could be "company for each other." The references came from people Marcia had heard of and attested to her "character and refinement."

Marcia wrote Mrs. Cannon to come and see her. But when Orville drove off with the letter to mail a sudden panic seized her. She wanted to tear the letter up and let the days go on as they had. She waved to Orville and even as she did it, she could feel how cool the air was on her hand. Soon it would be fall and then winter. She didn't dare try Providence another winter.

TWO

ARCIA sat in the parlor waiting. Mrs. Cannon had written that she would come for an interview on Wednesday, as near four as she could make it. Her neighbor's son would drive her over from Dedham. Marcia wore her dark voile dress, the one with the organdie collar and cuffs trimmed with tatting, and her comb with the turquoises set in gold that her husband had given her to hold up the cascade of brown curls she had then. Now the tortoise-shell teeth showed through the thin white hair. Some old people were so careless about appearances. She wanted Mrs. Cannon to see that she was different.

There was a bowl of nasturtiums on the marble-topped

table and the blue glass pitcher full of early asters on the pianola. Marcia had started to take up the maidenhair ferns for winter and the finest of them, in a brass pot, stood on the square rosewood piano in the parlor across the hall. The Bennington jug on the front step was filled with goldenrod, sign of fall and coming cold. There was not a speck of dust any place and Marcia had washed the kitchen floor that morning. The tea tray was ready with thin slices of brown bread. Mrs. Cannon should see that the "pleasant living" was true.

The front door stood open so she could hear the sound of the car and catch the first glimpse of Mrs. Cannon. She would know when she first saw her whether she could live with her. But Marcia felt uneasy. She couldn't keep her mind on anything and her eyes moved around these rooms trying to imagine someone here all the time. That showed what a state she had come to, living alone so long, she told herself. The house used to be full when they were all children at home, and she set her mind to peopling it again: Will and Matt coming in from the barn for dinner and her father sharpening his knife for carving the roast; she and Caroline helping their mother in the kitchen and perhaps some neighbor, perhaps even John when he was courting her, there for dinner. And Grandmother and Grandfather just beyond the wall that separated the main house from the southwest corner. The house had not seemed full then, just natural. It would be good to have someone else here; but her lips felt so dry she went out to the kitchen for a drink of water.

Just then the doorpull set the little bell behind the stairs jingling through the hall. As Marcia came in from the kitchen she saw Mrs. Cannon standing at the screen, a large woman leaning her head forward to peer into the house.

"How do you do, I'm Mrs. Bea Cannon." The woman announced herself as soon as she saw Marcia. "My, it's nice and cool in here!" Her voice was a little loud as though she thought Marcia must be deaf. She wasn't pretty; her face was too red, and her short gray hair was too frizzy, but 'she was neat. And she did have kind brown eyes. Marcia tried not to be disappointed. Mrs. Cannon sat down by the window and her eyes traveled around the room.

Sitting across from her, Marcia felt small. She cleared her throat and made her voice a little louder to bring Mrs. Cannon's attention back to her.

"I realize that this is a rather strange arrangement. . ." Marcia began.

"Why, I don't think so at all. I think it's real sensible. Naturally, you're lonely and want someone to keep you company."

"No," Marcia said slowly. "I'm not really lonely. I've lived alone a long time and I keep busy, but I think I should have someone with me . . ." Her voice trailed off. She couldn't bring herself to say "in case I become sick," "in case I should die suddenly," "someone to carry wood and keep the fires." "But I would want it to be a very independent arrangement," she said.

Mrs. Cannon broke in. "That's the way with my neighbor in Dedham and me. She goes her way and I go mine, but she's there when I want to call over to her."

Marcia felt reassured. "And, as you see, I have plenty of room here."

Mrs. Cannon nodded. "This is a pretty place; you'd never expect to find a place kept up like this way up on top of this hill. Do you have much land with it?"

Marcia took her outside to show her where the boundary ran. It seemed easier to talk outdoors.

"You've got quite a woodlot there."

"Yes, but I have an arrangement with Orville Greenstead . . ." She explained about the lower acre carefully. It must all be very clear.

"I have woodbine on my barn, too," Mrs. Cannon said as they came back to the house. "And my clematis vine is just beautiful. You'll have to see it sometime." Marcia was glad that she liked growing things.

As they went upstairs, Marcia could hear Mrs. Cannon breathing heavily behind her.

"I s'pose these stairs don't bother you, you're so thin,

but I'm fleshy. It don't seem to make any difference how little I eat," Mrs. Cannon explained.

They looked at each of the four bedrooms. Marcia kept them all open in summer with the beds covered with hand-pieced quilts her mother had made.

"You must have had these things a good long while!" Mrs. Cannon said, touching the high dresser in the front bedroom.

"Quite a while," Marcia said.

"I see you've only got one stove upstairs."

"In the west bedroom there's a register over the sitting room stove. The heat comes up through that."

"Do you burn coal?"

"No, we have so much wood."

They went through the rooms downstairs.

"Oh, you've got tea ready!" Mrs. Cannon said with pleasure when she saw the tray. She started to pull out the chair at the kitchen table, but Marcia picked up the tray.

"I thought we'd take it in the sitting room. The sun comes in there this time in the afternoon."

"I just thought it would save you steps. Here, let me; you're such a little mite." Mrs. Cannon took the tray out of her hands and Marcia came behind bringing the pitcher of hot water.

Over tea Marcia said, "I wouldn't want to have some-

43

one come up here who had never lived in the country. It would seem too far away."

"Oh, I love the country," Mrs. Cannon said. "But you take city folks, why, they'd go crazy up here. You must be a good cook, Mrs. Elder. This brown bread is delicious."

Marcia had a second cup of tea to put off saying the final word. She just didn't know . . .

Mrs. Cannon finished before she did and picked up the crumbs from her lap, one by one.

"Well, it's agreeable to me," she said briskly. "That is, if it is to you," she added. "We'd have our little differences, I suppose, that's human nature, but I guess you and me could get along."

Again that panic rose in Marcia's mind. If she said yes this woman whom she had never seen before today would be here all the time, as long as she lived. She glanced over at her, at her plain red face framed by the curly hair, her figured silk dress that stopped a little too far above the thick ankles, but she had a kind face; she sounded cheerful. The minister in Dedham had written that she was "a fine churchwoman, intelligent, thrifty and pleasant."

Marcia looked out the window across the grass. It was already littered with leaves from the elm tree by the wall. But when had they fallen? Then she remembered she had been too busy in the house this week to notice.

"Pieces of gold," her father used to call them. But the leaves in the grass weren't gold. They were only dull yellow and brown without the sun on them. Just while they were sitting there the sun had left the lawn and moved up the hill back of the house.

Mrs. Cannon reached over and took her teacup. "Shall I just take these things out to the kitchen for you?"

"Oh, thank you," Marcia said. She might suggest that they try it for a month. Mrs. Cannon could come and see; she could see . . . but that was shilly-shallying. "Fish, cut bait, or go ashore," her father always said.

Marcia stood up, holding on to the arms of the chair because she felt so trembly. "Yes, it's agreeable to me." She swallowed quickly to get rid of the dryness in her throat that choked her.

"I suppose we should have it all in writing, but we don't need to bother with that now," Mrs. Cannon said.

"I'll have it all written out by the time you come. Orville Greenstead will take me down to have it witnessed by the town clerk." Marcia's eyes seemed to lose all color when she faced so squarely to the light. She went with Mrs. Cannon to the car and shook her hand.

"I know I'm going to love it here, Mrs. Elder; it seems so peaceful and quiet. You and I'll have a real good time together and I'll take good care of you. You might as well call me Bea now as later."

"Thank you," Marcia answered but she didn't offer

to be called Marcia. She had been Mrs. Elder for so many years she had come to think of herself as Mrs. Elder.

With her hand on the door of the car, Bea Cannon paused. "I meant to ask you, Mrs. Elder, what room would I have? I like a warm bedroom. Perhaps I better have that room with the stove in it."

"I guess that will be all right," Marcia said. "That was always Mother's room," she added, but the car had already started.

THREE

MARCIA had plenty to do that week before Mrs. Cannon arrived. She hardly went outside the house except to hang some yellowed sheets on the line and air the blankets and quilts. One day she moved her mother's Boston rocker across the hall into the other bedroom and substituted a different one. She took the family pictures off the wall in that bedroom but the sun had faded the wallpaper so she had to find others to cover the places. She wrapped a dozen coin silver teaspoons and the pearl-handled knives in their flannel cases and locked them in the bottom drawer of the dining room dresser, but after she had taken out the key she sat still on the floor. Then she put the key back in the lock. They would all be Mrs. Cannon's some day, anyway, so she might as well leave everything where it was.

Marcia had Orville Greenstead fit the storm windows on the house early this year and when he was fixing those in the upstairs bedrooms she told him she was going to have someone stay with her, but she only said "this winter."

Orville laid his screw-driver down on the dresser. "Well, Mrs. Elder, I'm glad to hear it. You've done the sensible thing."

And that was what she told herself a dozen times a day, but she felt uneasy. She forgot and left the cat in the house all night and took the sugar-bowl down cellar instead of the cream. She was glad nobody was there to see how foolish and absent-minded she was.

After supper, the night before Mrs. Cannon came, Marcia lit the lamp in the parlor and sat down at the piano. The pianola wouldn't do tonight. She played *God of Our Fathers,* fumbling a little over the chords. That had been her brother Will's favorite and it was firm enough to put strength into anyone, but it tired her and she didn't play the second verse. She blew out the light and went to sit on the front doorstep before bed.

There was no hint of winter in the air. The warm Indian summer night came close enough almost to touch. She heard a rustling in the grass that must be a toad going about his mysterious errands in the dark, and once she heard a sleepy peeping in the big Maples. There was the sound of the brook back of the house. It always seemed to run faster in the fall, but tonight it was in no hurry at all. She was in no hurry either.

Orville said he'd seen a deer yesterday when he went to chop wood. She wished she could see it. The night was very still. The woodbine against the house hung as motionless as though it were still green. She walked down the road in the dark with her arms folded over her shawl. She would always have this. She would be housebound a little time in the winter, but there was the fall and spring and summer. This way, having someone here, she would go on in her own house as long as she lived. It didn't matter if it all went to Mrs. Cannon when she was through with it. Comforted, she went in to bed.

Marcia waited downstairs while Mrs. Cannon—Bea— "freshened up" after her trip over from Dedham. It was rather nice to have someone stirring around upstairs.

"I imagine this is a cold house in winter with all these windows. I've got a mind to make sandbags to lay along the sills." Bea's voice came down the stairs ahead of her. "I notice these storm windows don't fit real tight."

"No, it's a very warm house. It's well made and it's

brick, you know," Marcia said. "And we don't have to worry about running out of wood."

Bea sat down across the table from her and took out her fancy work.

"That's pretty," Marcia said, nodding at her handi-work.

"Yes, it's about the prettiest pattern I've ever done. I don't believe you could do it, though. It'd be too hard on your eyes at your age," Bea said. Marcia didn't answer. She turned to her knitting.

"You must miss church up here. I was always active in church work in Dedham; president of the King's Daughters two years running, and chairman of the church suppers and all that," Bea said.

"Sometime you can get Orville Greenstead to drive you down to church, but he charges for it, of course, and when the weather's bad he's afraid of the hill."

At five, Marcia went out to start supper, explaining that she always liked to eat early.

"I'll just come out and watch you and get the lay of the land; but I'm not one to set by and let others work," Bea told her.

Marcia was so used to doing things alone it confused her to have Bea watching.

"Gracious, you make hard work of poaching eggs; just drop 'em right in your boiling water, you don't need to slide 'em off a saucer. Here, let me show you!"

Bea had them ready before Marcia had the toast made. "This is wild strawberry jam," Marcia told Bea when they were seated at the dining room table. "It's made without any heat but the sun. I always sun-preserve a few for special occasions; the berries plump out and don't mash up the way they do when you cook them."

Bea tasted it critically, a little on the tip of a spoon. "A bit on the sweet side for me. In Dedham, the Ladies' Aid had an expert give a lecture on canning and she said you really weren't safe putting up fruit unless you cooked it at a rolling boil at least fifteen minutes."

Marcia sat up later than usual, hating to admit that she usually went to bed at eight, but she grew sleepy at the usual time. Bea went on about Dedham and the King's Daughters and how convenient her bungalow there was, until Marcia scarcely listened. When she took her lamp and said good night, Bea's words followed her out in the hall.

"I don't know whether I can get used to kerosene lamps after electricity. No bathroom is the worst cross. I have a fine bathroom in my house in Dedham. That's one thing I wouldn't be without."

By the time Marcia had brushed back her white hair and rolled it around her kid-curlers, and put on her high-necked gown she told herself she had just lived too long alone. She had grown too used to silence, and she lay down determined to be sensible and not borrow trouble.

But Bea didn't take easily to life on the hill.

"You mean you sometimes don't see a soul from one day's end to the next?" she asked incredulously.

Marcia nodded. "Today Orville Greenstead is coming over with a load of wood and I'm going to have him fix that blind on the east side that makes such a noise. We'll have to give him lunch, or I always do, but he's not much of a hand to talk," Marcia told her with a little gleam of mischief in her eye. Marcia had been a tease years ago.

But when she came back from the pasture where she had gone to look for partridge berries she found Bea sitting in the woodshed visiting with Orville. Orville was unloading wood in a desultory fashion, stopping to talk between times. He went to work more briskly when he saw Marcia, and Bea took her pan of potatoes and went on into the kitchen.

"You might set Orville's dinner on the kitchen table and we'll take something light out on the south side of the house and eat it. We won't have many more warm days like this," Marcia said.

But Bea said, "That makes lots of steps and I've got a good hot dinner cooked up. Mr. Greenstead brought a head of cabbage with him and I boiled it with a piece of side-pork."

So the three of them sat down to eat in the kitchen.

The heat from the big range fanned their faces instead of the breeze from the hill. The large old kitchen was pleasant enough with its windows on two sides, the red bricked-in fireplace back of the range, the gray soapstone sink and the wide blue boards of the floor, but Marcia had counted on eating out where the shadow of the elm tree met the shadow of the eaves and the sun lay across the grass. The sharp smell of the pork and cabbage dulled her appetite and she had to make herself eat half the serving Bea put on her plate. She hadn't eaten heavy meals in so long they didn't set well.

"You need to be fed up a little; you're as thin as a sparrow in winter," Bea said.

"I've always been thin," Marcia protested, "my mother's people were all thin and my father's too."

"Well, it isn't healthy to be as skinny as you are; one good wind could blow you away. I'm going to see you're taken care of now." And Bea laid her arm around Marcia's shoulders.

Gradually Bea took over the work of housekeeping.

"It won't take me any time," Bea would say and the efficiency of her tone brushed Marcia aside. When Marcia suggested making a loaf of brown bread or muffins from the canned blueberries she had put up last summer Bea said, "Oh, don't you bother. I can do it in half the time." And she could, but things didn't taste the same.

55

Bea liked to do things her way and Marcia didn't like to protest. It seemed ungrateful when Bea was so willing. After all, it wasn't as though she paid Bea a salary, she told herself, walking over to the sugar-bush or down toward the spring so she wouldn't be in the way. Bea was good-natured and a good housekeeper and she was fortunate to have her.

Bea had certain rules for saving work; she believed in keeping the table "set up" in the kitchen so there wasn't "that to do over every meal," which interfered with Marcia's way of eating where the sun fell.

"My goodness, Mrs. Elder, you'd think the sun wasn't ever going to come up again, the way you follow it around!"

"I like the sun," Marcia murmured.

Another of Bea's rules had to do with saving bed linen. "You can't tell me that two women, sleeping alone and bathing every Saturday night, need to change their sheets every week; once in two weeks is enough."

Marcia heard this dictum in silence but with her own mental reservations. That Saturday morning, while Bea was talking to Orville in the front of the house, Marcia emptied the two tea kettles into the wash-tub and filled it up with the warm water from the reservoir in the stove. The scallops of yellow soap gave off a strong aromatic smell, and worked up a fine suds. Marcia plunged her sheet up and down in the soapy water, dripping a little on the floor as she lifted it into the second tub. She was almost through when Bea came back to the kitchen.

"Mrs. Elder!" Bea said sharply from the door. Her red face showed exasperation. Her glance took in the water on the floor, the emptied tea kettles, Marcia wringing the sheet in the sink.

Bea took hold of the sheet with capable hands. Marcia held on tightly. The two women stood side-by-side.

"I like a fresh sheet every week and two of them in summer," Marcia said. A flush appeared high on her usually pale face.

"Well, there's no sense in it. Wait till you get to the stage where you need one every day!" Bea said.

The flush deepened. Marcia jerked the sheet. "I'll do this, myself, thank you!"

"Mrs. Elder, now don't go getting yourself worked up. Just let go and I'll finish it; you're making a mess all over the kitchen!"

With sudden, frantic strength Marcia pulled the whole wet mass against her and carried it dripping outside. She could feel the water soaking the front of her dress. Let it! She fastened the sheet over the line and its quick billowing out in the wind, like a flag, was justification and triumph. Then she went back into the house.

Bea was wiping up the floor. "You know, Mrs. Elder, I wouldn't mind so much; nobody can ever say that Bea

Cannon ever minded work, but you'll come down sick if you carry on like that. You aren't as strong as you once were."

Marcia went silently into her bedroom and shut the door. Bea wrote letters at the kitchen table on the side where a place wasn't set. No more was said, but Bea washed Marcia's sheet once a week after that.

Orville's car came more often now to bring the things Bea ordered from the store. Marcia didn't like eating so much meat but Bea said, "I bought it with my own money and it's all cooked; you might as well eat it. My folks were always good meat eaters." And often when Orville brought the groceries, Bea said to Marcia, "I've asked Orville to stay and eat with us; a man alone don't ever cook right for himself."

It was a source of wonder to Marcia that Bea could keep so busy. With only the two of them to do for she kept her days so full she never had time to go for a walk. "You go ahead, Mrs. Elder; I've got so much to do here I don't know where to start!" she often said when Marcia asked her to go up the hill with her.

And every night she had her letter-writing to friends in Dedham. Marcia came to know a certain Hattie Carew, who lived next door to Bea in Dedham, as well as Bea herself.

Bea was always setting a distinction between herself and Marcia.

"You see, Mrs. Elder, you're past eighty and the old live in the past, but I've got to keep my fingers and my wits busy or I'd go crazy off up here. I'd just like to take you down to my snug little bungalow in Dedham. My! you could be cozy there. It's got hot air heat and electricity and running . . ."

But Marcia was not listening. She had heard all this so many times before. Perhaps she did live in the past. She often went outside and in the rooms in the southwest corner that hadn't been lived in since her Grandfather Wyman died. Their very separateness made them a refuge to her when the rest of the house was filled with the sound of Bea's housekeeping. But in November she stayed there too long and caught a bad cold. Bea put her to bed and dosed her steadily.

"The idea of your moping off in that closed-off corner of the house when it's down to freezing outside; some folks would think you were touched."

Marcia submitted docilely to Bea's care. It was good to lie still and have things done for her and she didn't have to listen to the steady stream of conversation. But at night when she couldn't sleep Bea's words came back to her. She wasn't as strong as she once was. And she wondered if she *were* a little touched. She remembered Miss Squires who used to live alone in the house at the top of the hill. People said she was touched because she talked to herself. As a child Marcia was always afraid

59

to meet her after dark and walked way over in the ditch so the whole road lay between them. How cruel children were! But the shadow of a fear lurked in her mind and left her less sure of herself, almost apologetic about what she did.

Bea had soon tired of carrying wood for her bedroom stove and lugging down the ashes, and when Marcia was sick she moved downstairs and slept on the couch in the dining room, close to the heater. Marcia couldn't come out of her room at night now without waking Bea. Bea would sit up in bed and ask sleepily, "What's the matter, Mrs. Elder? Are you sick?"

And there was no need to put a stick in the stove, Bea packed it tight with great chunks of wood before she went to bed. Marcia missed her cup of tea she used to make in the night and she felt suffocated in such close quarters, but Bea said, "There isn't any sense in heating the whole house; these three rooms are plenty this weather." She closed off the sitting room and parlor and hall with sandbags against the doors to keep out the draughts and they lived in the kitchen, dining room and Marcia's bedroom.

"It gets too close to be healthy," Marcia protested.

"That's what you thought when you caught cold and took sick!" Bea reminded her. "A person might think we were crazy, two women off up here on a deserted hillside. It would make a feature story in the Sunday

Suppl'ment if those reporters ever got ahold of it. I was telling Orville that," Bea said.

Marcia coughed and felt weak and tired.

Orville kept on coming even when there were no errands. He sat in the kitchen and talked to Bea while she worked, or Bea talked to him. Marcia could hear Bea's voice going on and on and Orville's coming in briefly only now and then.

FOUR

EA LOOKED sharply at Mrs. Elder sitting in a chair by the kitchen window. Her hands were quiet in her lap. She seemed to be watching something, but Bea stood behind her and there was nothing to see but the snow-covered yard and the stone wall and the bare branches of a tree.

"I don't know what you see to look at. It just looks cold to me," Bea said.

Mrs. Elder didn't answer, which irritated Bea. She did that more and more. Bea wondered if Mrs. Elder were failing; if she might not just "go off" some day and she'd come in and find her "gone." The thought made Bea nervous. She buttoned her sweater all the way to the neck and put another stick of wood in the stove. Then she got her crocheting.

"I never could bear to sit with my hands idle. How you can stand it, I'm sure I don't know!"

"I don't stand. I sit down to it," Marcia said, her face crinkling into a smile.

Bea jerked her head in annoyance. Her mouth tightened. Who'd ever expect Mrs. Elder to pick her up like that. But it was better than having her sit like a statue.

"All right, sitting then. If there was anything to see I could understand your sitting there, but there isn't a car or a wagon going by the house week in, week out. Not a mortal thing to make you look out the window."

Marcia laughed. There were things: today it thawed a little and would freeze again by four o'clock. There were chickadees in the bush by the barn and yesterday she heard a jay scream down by the brook, even if she couldn't see him. The willows on the bank were yellow-brown as molasses in the sun. She was watching for the brook to show through any day now. First it would look like a dark chain dragged across the snow, then the dark links would widen and turn green, like a necklace. . . .

"What are you laughing at?" Bea asked crossly. "If you'd carried wood all winter and cared for a sick woman in the bargain, you wouldn't see anything to laugh at!"

Marcia forgot why she had laughed. She watched a rabbit hopping across the snow. It was comical the way

66

it froze once, pretending it was a stone, but she didn't point it out even though Bea hadn't seen it.

"Mrs. Elder, I been thinking; why wouldn't it be a fine thing for you to sell off your things next summer? If you had the auction in the summer when there were tourists around, and got Sam Wilson from over Dedham way for the auctioneer, you'd get quite a bit for some of these old things of yours. Then you could come to live with me in Dedham."

Marcia sat without speaking. She could feel Bea looking at her. She twisted her wedding-ring on her finger, and moistened her lips, they felt so dry. Finally she said:

"I shouldn't ever like to give up my home."

Bea didn't mention it again all through the spring, but there it lay between them.

June came and Marcia was outdoors again whenever it was warm enough. Now Bea will forget about the winter, Marcia told herself, but Bea kept on fretting about her house in Dedham. She wondered whether the folks she had rented it to had taken care of it. She talked about having it painted and Orville said he'd do the job for nothing if she furnished the paint. One day Bea and Orville drove off to Dedham for the day.

"I hate to leave you, but I s'pose you'll be all right," Bea said.

"Oh, yes. You've left food enough to last a fortnight," Marcia answered, smiling to herself about that Spring day last year when she had gone to sleep on the hill and waked up in a snowstorm.

She was glad to be alone. She made a loaf of brown bread, humming as she moved around her own kitchen again. She got down on her knees and pruned around the rose bushes. Bea said that was too hard for an old lady. And she opened the front door of the house and propped it there with the conch shell to let the air stream through. The June sun fell on the faces of her grandparents, painted in oil and framed with wide gold borders, and seemed to soften their cracked visages.

She put on a coat and went into the parlor to play some tunes on the old square piano, but instead she sat quietly on the stool, her feet on the rug she had hooked so long ago to save the carpet from wearing. The stillness and peace seemed so good. And she ate her lunch on a tray out on the doorstep and fed bits of it to a squirrel.

She could never leave this place and go to Dedham. Why, she would sooner be dead. If Bea wanted to go back to her own place, they would break off their arrangement. Here, alone, she felt strong and sure she could manage by herself. The June sun was warm at noon on the south side of the house. A patch of new grass flamed bright green around the old stone carriage block. It was an earlier season than last year.

Bea didn't come till after dark. Marcia watched for the lights of Orville's car coming up the road a long while before she saw them. It was nice having someone to watch for again, she admitted to herself. She remembered how she and Caroline used to watch for her father's carriage coming up the hill, the lantern swinging underneath. Even now she could remember how they used to dart off to catch a ride the rest of the way to the barn . . . so long ago, almost seventy-five years ago, but her mind discarded the passage of time.

Bea was in rare good spirits. She sat down by the stove and ate the supper Marcia had saved for her, telling Marcia all about her friends in Dedham between mouthfuls.

"Was your house in good condition?" Marcia asked.

"Just fine, but I was glad to have the tenants go and give it a good cleaning and Orville's going to start in painting next week. He's going to live right there while he does it." Bea broke off with a short laugh that was almost a giggle. "Mrs. Elder, I don't know how you'll take it, and they do say that there's no fool like an old one, but we up and did it today!"

Marcia frowned, trying to understand. Bea was so excited and in such good spirits, but her words didn't make sense. Bea looked different, too. Her face was flushed, and her hair was mussed by her hat and softer around her face than she usually wore it. Suddenly Bea held out her hand and Marcia saw the wedding ring.

69

"You and . . . and Orville Greenstead?" Marcia asked incredulously.

Bea nodded. "It just seemed a sensible arrangement. Now you'll have two of us to take care of you and there'll be a man around the house to do the heavy work."

Marcia couldn't think of anything to say at first. All life seemed to be nothing but arrangements, decided upon by people of great good sense, not outgrowth of time and feeling.

"I knew it'd be a shock to you, Mrs. Elder, that's why I didn't tell you beforehand. We've been talking about it all spring. 'Course Orville'll put what he has toward expenses and what with doing the man's work there is to do around he'll pay his way. Just look how he's painting my house; that would cost two hunderd and fifty dollars easily if I had to pay to have it done and . . ."

Marcia went across the room to the cistern and dipped herself a drink of water. The water was ice-cold, running from the spring on the hill. It seemed to cleanse her mouth of an unpleasant taste.

"I hope you'll be happy, Bea," she said slowly.

But Bea went on with her talk of arrangements. "Orville will be busy at Dedham for a good ten days and then he has his own place to take care of and see about selling, if anybody'll buy it. He wants to stay on there through haying . . ." Bea paused. "And then we don't feel it's fair, Mrs. Elder, with you not knowing and all, to live up here when our arrangement was only for you and me." There was a longer pause. "So . . . we think it would be best if, in the fall or maybe late summer, we all moved down to my place in Dedham."

"Perhaps it would be best, all things considered, Bea, if you and Orville went to live together and left me here alone," Marcia said. It angered her that her voice trembled.

"Now, Mrs. Elder, that's one thing we won't hear to. I won't have anybody saying Bea Cannon ever made an agreement and didn't stick to it! But there, we've got lots of time to talk about moving, later. Goodness! It's near ten o'clock and way past your bedtime."

"I'll have to think about it. That wasn't our agreement," Marcia said.

But Marcia slept uneasily as though a weight lay on her mind.

FIVE

THERE were bad electric storms toward the end of the summer. One close, still day followed another; the morning sun glared down as bright as Marcia's brass jardiniere. By afternoon the clouds piled up in a dark mass and the leaves on the Maples and Elms drooped as though rain would fall any minute. But the minutes passed without any rain, and the heat and tension grew silently . . . like the contending wills of two women . . . till the very timbers of the barn seemed ready to burst into flame. Thunder, when it came, made the tension audible. And lightning, cracking the skies apart in branching lines like the roots of trees, made it visible.

"My goodness, I believe storms are worse off here on this old hill than any place I ever see them." Bea's voice came down the stair well punctuated by the slamming of a window. "You know you left your bedroom window wide open, Mrs. Elder, and the rain would have come in like death and destruction all over your floor. Like as not, it would have dripped down through the ceiling if I hadn't gone to see." Bea looked accusingly in the doorway of the kitchen where Marcia had been sitting, but her chair was empty.

"Mrs. Elder!" Bea called. She opened the kitchen door and called out through the woodshed. Only thunder, so close it seemed to roll off the shed roof, answered her. Bea retreated quickly into the kitchen and closed the door to shut out the storm, but lightning forced its way into the room, even to the dark place behind the stove. Bea stood with her back against the door. Her face was the gray color of the yeast soaking in a cup on the sinkboard. It scared her to be here alone in a storm.

The rain came with a rush, pouring against the windows so you couldn't see across the yard. But the lightning and thunder kept up just the same. Where was Mrs. Elder? Exasperation edged Bea's tone as she called her. She went back through the house and called up the stairs just as the thunder came again, drowning out her voice. Lightning illuminated the hall and the unfriendly looking faces of the portraits on either side of the front

76

door. Bea cowered against the stair rail and closed her eyes so as not to see the light. What if it struck that big elm in the corner of the yard; it would crash down on the house and kill them all.

"Mrs. Elder! Where are you?" Fear made her voice shrill. She climbed the stairs again to look under the high bed in Marcia's room and went out to the toilet and down to the cellar where the booming of the thunder seemed to come from the depths of the earth. Wouldn't a person be safer there? Only you'd catch cold and there would be mice running over your feet.

Bea was so out of breath when she came back to the kitchen she leaned against the sink for a minute. Mrs. Elder had been right here in the kitchen when she went upstairs, sitting there in the rocker by the window. If she took a notion to go out in a storm like this she *was* getting childish, just as she'd told Orville. He couldn't see it, but he would when she told him about this stunt! Bea went out to the hall closet to see if Mrs. Elder's cape was there. It was, but her cane was gone.

There was anger in the hurried movements of her hands as Bea buttoned her raincoat and pulled on her rubbers. Anger brought some color back into her cheeks. The thunder was drawing back across the hills but the lightning was still too sharp to be comfortable and Bea waited a few minutes in the shed. The rain was more than coming down, but there was nothing for it but to

77

go and hunt for Mrs. Elder. After all, she was here to look after her and how would it look if Mrs. Elder was found dead out in the storm? Bea phrased it to herself as she would later phrase it to Hattie Carew in her letter.

She crossed the yard and looked up and down the grass-grown road and beyond at the dripping woods. Once she called and her voice cracked but was mercifully covered over by the thunder.

"I tell you I was nearly wild," she would tell Hattie Carew, "but I thought it wouldn't help any for me to catch cold and be sick, myself, so I started back to the house. I was going past the barn when I happened to look up toward the pasture and, sitting there on the stone wall, calm as you please, with her back to me, was Mrs. Elder!"

"Mrs. Elder! Mrs. Elder!" Bea screamed. Marcia turned and waved. She had on the big straw hat that usually hung in the shed and the rain rolled off the brim.

Bea stood where she was and called again. "You'll be sick if you stay out in that rain." Mrs. Elder acted simpleminded. She came slowly down the hill with that snake-headed cane of hers as though there wasn't any rain at all. She stopped once and looked at the sky.

The thunder was further away now and the lightning was only a sudden quick illumination as though some giant match was struck and flamed an instant before going out.

"Quite a storm!" Marcia said when she came up to Bea.

"I should think it was and you scared me out of a year's growth," Bea retorted. "I went all over the house and barn, even down in the cellar." Bea's eyes flashed and her head jerked as she spoke. "I was afraid you'd got hurt or something. I was so worried I could hear my heart pound louder than the thunder. What were you trying to do?"

"I saw the storm coming over the hill and I just thought I'd walk out in it," Marcia said quietly.

"In all that lightning! Plenty of folks have been struck down dead by lightning. There was a man fixing his fence about two miles north of Dedham . . . I knew his daughter . . . and he . . ."

"I'm not afraid of lightning any more," Marcia said, interrupting Bea as though she hadn't heard her. There was something about the tone of Mrs. Elder's voice that made Bea glance at her. "Her face was as white as a cold storage chicken and wet from the rain; and her lips set that way made her look like a witch. But it was her eyes that were the worst; they were pale and cold as a cat's," Bea would write Hattie Carew.

"Lightning won't strike me," Marcia said. "I've given it plenty of chances since it killed my husband sixty-six years ago."

A shocked little gasp came from Bea. "Where was he at?" she asked with immediate relish for details.

"In bed beside me," Marcia Elder said. She nodded toward the woods. "Look over there, the storm's about over and it hasn't rained enough to do much good. I think I'll walk up the road a ways."

Bea stood and watched her go without a word. "I tell you," she wrote Hattie Carew that night, "Mrs. Elder gave me the creeps. I wanted to ask her more about it and where they were living but I couldn't seem to bring the subject around again. She's close-mouthed when she feels like it. In a way, she's not real good company because she's so silent at times. I'm thankful I'm moving back to Dedham in the fall, with Orville to live with us. Mrs. Elder hasn't *said* she would but she knows very well she can't live up here alone another winter so I guess she'll have to."

SIX

MARCIA ELDER was so quiet standing in the doorway to the parlor that early comers to the auction scarcely noticed her. The auctioneer was already here. People, the summer folk, and the children and grandchildren of town-people she had always known, were filling the chairs that covered the side lawn. The legs of their chairs would dig holes, like small graves, in the green grass, but the grass no longer mattered. Tonight the grass would be sold with the house.

She had come in once more to see the parlor as it had always been, to fix it in her mind so that she could close her eyes always and see it as it was now; her wedding picture and John's against the gold and blue wall paper, the picture of Abraham Lincoln, the two mirrors, one gold-framed with a schoolhouse at the top, the other mahogany . . . Bea said the mirrors ought to bring a pretty price . . . the haircloth sofa, the spring rocker, upholstered in gold-colored plush, that was newer than the rest of the things in the room, the marble-topped table . . . Her eyes saw even the conch shell that served as a doorstop.

She thought how she had made the hooked rug under the piano stool to protect the flowered Axminster and now the rest of the carpet had faded and the hooked rug could never be moved. She was like that hooked rug. A wave of anguish rose in her throat. She took hold of the shining white door jamb to steady herself.

These were her things. She was being separated from them. She hadn't thought Bea could do a thing like this when it came right down to it. Why hadn't she put her foot down and told Bea no? But Bea had so many arguments, and Bea kept at her so. And she was tired of talking. It couldn't be for long; she was eighty-four now. As Bea said, she wasn't as strong as she used to be. Sometimes, she was dizzy when she stood up quickly. It bothered her more to think about the cold this winter. Bea said her house kept a nice even heat all over. . . .

The auctioneer was beginning. He had taken his place on the doorstep on the north side of the house. Orville would be coming in soon to strip the house, taking things out one by one.

Marcia went back to the kitchen that was so big and sunny. The china was packed in bushel baskets to be auctioned off, a pig in a poke, some good things in with the ordinary dishes. They went faster that way, Bea said. There was her brown teapot that her grandmother had made tea in. She stooped and touched it lovingly. The curve of the handle seemed to fit her hand. The lid was always a little top-heavy so she had been careful to hold it when she poured tea. She hadn't needed to be so careful all these years. What good was it now? It was funny she didn't feel worse about selling her things. She just felt cold and kind of shaky and faraway.

"Mrs. Elder, there isn't any sense in your getting all worked up and nervous. Why don't you go up on the hill till the auction's over, unless you feel like lying down." Bea's voice was busy. Underneath the busyness it had a kind of excitement in it. Often, just the way she talked made Marcia feel useless. She didn't answer Bea sometimes, but today she said:

"No, I'll stay right here."

That was the least she could do for these old things that she had known all her life. She went out to sit in the shed where she could watch the auction from the open lattice door. She sat in the rocker that had been her mother's, that Bea had said she might as well keep, she set such a store by it. Bea didn't mean to be unkind. Sitting in the rocker that was going with her to Bea's house, Marcia felt less shaky. Hand-turned the rocker was, and rush-bottomed, the sort of thing the summer people were always trying to buy. It gave her a secret pleasure to sit in it to keep it.

She looked at the old settee that the auctioneer had in front of him. That settee had always stood in the shed here where she could sit on it to take off her rubbers. The shed seemed empty now without it. She closed her eyes and couldn't think what color it was. She opened them again and saw it for the first time as a settee, apart from its place in the woodshed. It was slate-colored. There had been rings of a different color once around the spindles, and it had a flower stenciled on the back that showed only faintly now. Perched up on the auctioneer's table the settee looked forlorn, its long row of spindles like the ribs of some clean carcass.

A woman's shrill voice called from the crowd, "What kind of wood is it?" Someone laughed because the question was irregular at an auction.

"Looks like genuine wood to me," the auctioneer drawled, and the crowd laughed. Marcia did not laugh.

The settee went to a woman who sat knitting through the auction. Her chauffeur came and carried the settee away. It was so long it had to go on top of the car.

Now they were bidding on the kitchen table and

chairs. Marcia wondered what she would miss most, the maple bed, or the cherry chest of drawers, or the drop-leaf table of apple-wood.

Bea fussed around her now and then. She could see how nervous Bea was. When she watched the auctioneer she kept pulling at her nose and now and then she smoothed back her hair.

Orville came through the shed. "He wants the parlor stuff next, Bea." Orville jerked his thumb at the auctioneer. He liked being busy and important. All his life Orville had gone at the beck and call of women; his mother until he was in his forties, now Bea. Marcia watched his faded blue shirt-back under the suspenders as he disappeared into the house. There was meekness in his line of shoulder and in the creased look of his thin neck, and she felt a kind of pity for him.

What kind of a life could he and Bea have? Wondering about them kept her away from the thought of living with them that had kept rising in her mind all summer like bitter heartburn. Bea smoothed his hair now and then and told him how spruce he looked when he was all dressed up, but more the way a woman talked to a pet cat than a husband.

Now they were auctioning off the haircloth sofa. The whatnot would go next. The bids were up to twenty-one dollars on the sofa. She could see Bea's eagerness from where she sat. Bea's nose projected out a little too far, like a dog's on scent.

Marcia had sat on that sofa and listened to Samuel Whitcomb propose, when she was eighteen, no, seventeen, and told him no. She could remember how the carved grape cluster on the arm of the sofa had felt to her fingers as she said the words, cool and smooth-polished and firm as a person's mind should be.

Her mind had not been like that the day John Elder had asked her to marry him and go west. It had been excited and a little fearful about going so far away, but happy about going with John.

"Maybe we'll never come back here, Marcia," John had said as they drove down Ryder hill after the wedding and she hadn't cared. But only a year later she had come back, alone, empty-armed. John had been struck dead by lightning in bed beside her, out on the ranch in Illinois. She had run out into the dark and stood there in the rain and lightning and thunder wanting to be killed, too. When the dark split open and the lightning showed up the log buildings of the ranch and the grasses that seemed as tall as bushes, and the stones, queer and white and sudden, she hadn't closed her eyes. For the first time in her life she wasn't afraid of a storm. But nothing happened.

She could remember the day she had come back to the valley and driven up to the hill farm. It had been in

August, a day like this. Along the road the grass was dusty and Father said it had been a hot summer. Mother was waiting for her at the front door.

It didn't hurt any more to remember these things. It bothered her that it didn't, but they had happened so long ago. She looked coolly back to the auctioneer. The square piano was going. How pretty the rosewood case was! The piano had stood in the parlor that day she came back.

At first, she had lived here, with her hair up on her head and wearing black dresses as sober as her mother's, visiting her married sister and helping the neighbors with their babies. And then she had gone to teaching spelling and penmanship and needle-work in the seminary at Alden. That was when she had bought the player-piano.

"My, Mrs. Elder, I'm pleased to get that whatnot of yours; seems I've always envied that," Clara Breen stopped to tell her.

Folks from the village were all kind. They were sorry to see her leave the hill. She knew they felt Bea wasn't doing right to marry and get her to leave, but they were not close to her, a generation or so younger. She didn't discuss her affairs with anyone. And she was too tired to hold out against Bea any longer.

The piano went for sixty dollars, Clara Breen told her. Marcia's father had paid two hundred for it. "One of the city folks bought it to make into one of those darling old desks," Clara said.

It hurt Marcia to think of all the ivory and black keys being ripped out. It seemed as though sound belonged with the rich graining of the wood. The colors of the wood flowed across the case like music.

The walnut center-table with the marble top went for a dollar. Nobody wanted those any more. And the spring rocker brought a dollar and a half, but the blue glass match hat brought three-fifty.

"Don't you want to go in now, Mrs. Elder?" Bea asked. Marcia could see that it worried Bea to have her sit and watch her things sold. But she shook her head.

"Then I'll go get your shawl; it's cool out here."

Marcia let her lay it around her shoulders. Bea did thoughtful things like that. Orville did, too. They meant well enough. This hill farm seemed a lonely place to them, away from town, hard to heat and keep up, at least for a man like Orville, who was a better putterer than a farmer.

She watched the bedroom furniture go, all but her own bed that they had taken over to Bea's house with a load of fruit and trunks and things Bea wanted. Marcia remembered how smoothly the drawers of the highboy pulled and how the top drawer of the chest that used to stand in Matt's room always smelled of Macassar oil since the time he spilled the whole bottle in it. Remembering that, it was hard to believe that Matt had been dead thirty-two years.

And then the auction was over. The auctioneer came into the shed, hot and noisy, wiping the perspiration off his face. He went right by her, not knowing the things belonged to her. People were paying up at the table set under the crab-apple tree. Women did look happy when they'd bought something to take home. She could see it in the excited way they talked. That woman who had bid on half the things without getting anything finally looked petered out. The grass was all chewed up by feet and chairs and car wheels. She waited for Orville to come back to the shed.

"Orville, who got the farm?" How steady her voice was!

Orville shook his head. "There just ain't a soul would buy a farm way up here, Mrs. Elder, and the auctioneer thought we'd better just wait, so it wasn't put up."

She was glad about the farm. She had braced herself to hear. It was still hers, then. It would do her good down there in Bea's house to know she still owned her own home, even if it was empty. It was true that it was the only farm still occupied on Ryder hill, but when her grandfather built up here there were a dozen farms scattered along the ten miles between the county line and the covered bridge. Bea never had liked it. When she first came, Bea used to say it gave her the creeps to think of not a mortal soul to call to or borrow so much as a cup of sugar from. Bea never meant to stay up here long, in the first place, Marcia thought resentfully.

"Well, they've all gone!" Bea said. There was a triumphant air about her. She'd had her own way.

"It made me mad the things that didn't sell," Bea went on. "The pianola and the stoves, none except that old Franklin. 'Course, pianolas are 'way out of style. Nobody wants them any more now that they've got radios, but you'd have thought somebody would buy it. I told the auctioneer to take it along in his truck and sell it for what he could get, and I threw in those boxes and boxes of rolls you had."

Marcia didn't answer. She had had a good deal of pleasure out of that pianola. She wished they'd left it here.

"I guess you'll be glad of the quiet, Mrs. Elder. There was enough noise here today to make your head swim!" Bea said with relish. "Orville's still got these chairs to crate for some city folks. He'll have to spend another day or two up here. Doesn't it beat all, the old stuff that some of those folks'll ship across the country?"

Bea hurried in the house, still with the air of triumph about her. In a minute Marcia heard the sharp tap of her knife against the edge of the spider as she dropped bacon drippings into it. They would be having fried potatoes, most likely, something a little heartier than usual because of Orville. She was too tired to move. She sat there in her chair until Bea called her to supper.

At supper, Bea said without looking at her, "Orville says he can just as well drive over to Dedham tonight. We'd be there by nine if we went right along. 'Course, it's just up to you, but a house isn't very cheerful with empty rooms. Orville'll come back over and finish up tomorrow."

Marcia didn't answer. She could stand the trip so much better in the daylight. She had counted on another night here, even though her own bed was gone. There was no telling how soon, if ever, she would get back up here, and she had wanted to take a walk around the place again by herself. Bea had meant to go tonight, all the time. She might have told her that this morning!

"Of course, if you're too tired . . ." Bea began the way she did after she'd said what she meant to do.

"I guess I can do it," Marcia said. Perhaps the sooner the better. There was no use feeling resentful. When she had arranged with Bea to take care of her till she died she hadn't asked her to understand the way she felt about things. Suddenly, fiercely, she didn't want her to know. Nobody should. Her feelings were her own. She had arranged with Bea to come and take care of her because she was strong and capable and honest. She mustn't expect any more. It wasn't as though Bea Cannon were flesh and blood of hers.

And then they were driving down Ryder hill in the slow, creeping dusk. Orville let the car down over the thank-you-ma'ams the way you let a baby carriage down steps. Ryder hill wasn't a road that was meant for automobiles in the first place. The thank-you-ma'ams had been built into it to let the horses rest a little on the way. Now the county no longer bothered to keep the road up and witch grass and goldenrod grew in the middle. They stuck up boldly against the headlights of Orville's car, like the ghosts of flowers and grasses, like the grass on the prairie the night Marcia's husband was killed.

Orville and Bea were quiet driving. Bea was nervous about the road. She sat up straight and tense and gripped the side of the seat. Marcia sat in back. She had gone over this road too many times to be nervous.

It took too much strength to turn her head to try to look back up the hill and she was packed in with suitcases and the little old leather trunk she wanted to keep with her, full of old pictures, and odds and ends. She hadn't looked back the time she went away with John, either. She had been too happy.

But she knew without looking back how each curve in turn would close on the hill. How the house was standing dark and empty on its knoll. She had not cried.

She had only gone down the walk feeling tired and lonely.

The road seemed short tonight, shorter than she ever remembered it. Already she could see the lights from the village.

"We won't stop in the village unless you 'specially want to, Mrs. Elder?"

"No," Marcia said. What was there to stop for?

Bea settled herself more comfortably in the seat as they turned onto the state highway. Only sixteen more miles now to Dedham.

Marcia watched the road growing whiter as the dusk deepened; the string of cars, the fence posts. She did not let her mind go ahead to Dedham to Bea's house, nor back to her own house on the hill, just kept it there on the highway. Cars came toward them in a ceaseless procession, blare of bright light after bright light, blinding her so she couldn't see anything for seconds after, and then another, and another. . . . Marcia leaned back against the seat and closed her eyes.

Bea turned around to look at Marcia. "I guess she's dropped off to sleep," Bea said to Orville. "She didn't mind the way I thought she would. She didn't make any fuss at all. I wouldn't be surprised if, after she gets used to it, she'll like living in a village. Anyway, it wasn't Christian living off up there, two women alone!" Bea's voice that had held self-justification took on a coy note. Her shoulder inclined a little towards Orville's.

"And it'll be a relief not to have that big house to keep!" Bea said.

"It took a sight of wood to keep them stoves going all winter," Orville added.

Marcia listened from the back seat. Those two who were nothing to her talked so freely of what she minded and didn't mind. What did they know or care? Bea wanted rooms too hot. She liked doors shut and sand-bags along the cracks and window-ledges. Bea liked meat and potatoes for every meal but breakfast, and pie-crust made with too much flour, and vinegar on her vegetables. All the things that Bea did that she minded rose now in a heap.

Why hadn't she said she wouldn't leave her own home? Why had she let them auction everything off? She could have held Bea to her bargain. She could have sent Bea away . . . Bea had no right! Tears ran down her face, and she wiped them away with the back of her glove.

"Here we are!" Bea's voice triumphed. The car lights picked out the little bungalow, no bigger than three rooms of the old Wyman place.

Marcia was frightened looking at it, then, suddenly, tired, worn out with thinking and remembering and feeling. The cramped cottage was unimportant. Bea and Orville were unimportant. All her world, all her desires had shrunk to a craving for a warm, soft bed and a quiet room; not to talk, not to feel, just to be left alone. She dreaded the effort of getting out of the car, of the cold creeping up around her legs.

"First thing, we'll get you right to bed, Mrs. Elder," Bea said, coming back from unlocking the door. Her voice was capable. It went around Marcia like a warm coat. She let herself be wrapped in it. She was very tired . . . and old.

SEVEN

Marcia helped with the dishes mornings, wiping while Bea washed. Sometimes, Bea went out to talk to Hattie Carew who lived next door and Marcia hurried to get more done than Bea would expect. But it made her hands tremble when she hurried. When Bea's visit lasted so long that Marcia could get the dishes all done and put away she had a small, childish sense of achievement, even of triumph.

Marcia didn't feel as free here as in her own home. This was Bea's home. She "did" her own room, except when Bea advanced with mop and broom and dustpan and announced that she was going to give it a "good cleaning." Marcia always hurried in to lay the pictures and the little thermometer mounted on a shell and the russet leather sewing-case in the drawer till Bea was through.

"Don't you bother dusting; I can do those things," she always told Bea a little timidly.

And Bea would answer, reluctantly, like one whose nature it is to see a job, once started, through to the end. "Well, I don't know but it would give you something to do, as long as you're able, and you can sit down to it." Marcia felt she was more of a burden to Bea here.

"I hate to leave Mrs. Elder alone . . ." Marcia would hear Bea saying over the fence to Hattie Carew. "Of course, she's safe enough, but it's just the idea if she should fall or get a dizzy spell. After all, she's eighty-four."

It gave Marcia a queer feeling to hear herself talked about. She would sit on the little front porch with her hands in her lap and look at the blue veins that lay under the wrinkled tissue of her skin like twisted blue velvet ribbons. She was old. And gradually, sitting there, she lost interest in things. She would sit and doze without touching her knitting. What use was there in knitting another shawl when the one she had would outlive her?

She sat that fall and watched the maple leaves sifting down through the branches and wondered if she would live to see new green ones take their place. It wasn't that she felt any more feeble than she had for the last few years but that Bea's energy made her feel weaker by comparison. And Bea would look at her some days and say:

"My land, your color's poor! You ought to take a good tonic."

By the second week in November, it was too cold to sit out on the porch and then Marcia felt the cramped quarters of the bungalow more sharply. Bea turned on the radio right after breakfast.

"There, you can have something to listen to." And Marcia felt it too ungracious to object, but the radio rasped on her ears. There was so much talking over the radio and she was so far removed from an interest in beauty hints and new recipes, or the love affairs of some girl who wasn't so very much in love after all and wouldn't have needed to get into all that trouble if she'd had any sense. She liked tunes better but she seldom heard ones she knew on the radio.

Here in Bea's house that was filled with Bea's things, she missed her own possessions with a sharpness that she had not felt when she saw them go at the auction. But the meals bothered Marcia more than anything. Bea felt she must keep up a stream of conversation, taking in Orville and Marcia by turns.

"Mrs. Elder, I was talking to Hattie Carew this morning and she said she wished to goodness she knew where to buy an old-fashioned feather tick. 'My land,' I said,

'Mrs. Elder had one she'd have given away.' I guess it sold at the auction for around a dollar fifty, didn't it?"

Then it was Orville's turn, but when Bea spoke to Orville it was usually about something that ought to be done.

"Orville, I noticed you left those green tomatoes in the basket in the cellar without wrapping. You need to wrap every one separate or they'll rot on you."

Orville's jaws moving methodically on the baked beans was his only answer.

Marcia tried to separate herself from Bea and Orville and this table with the spotted tablecloth. She wished Bea would pull the shade halfway at noon. The sun came in too brightly on the ugliness and poverty of their comfortable living here.

When she was a child, she had watched her father and brothers butchering a pig. She had made herself look at the blood and the entrails and her father's wrists where the hairs were stained red with blood. She had not felt nauseated nor faint but infinitely separated from what her eyes saw and her nose smelled. She tried to feel that way now, sitting at the table with Bea and Orville. But she couldn't separate herself completely from their living because hers was a part of it.

"Mrs. Elder!" Bea's voice was sharp. "You must've been half asleep. I spoke to you three times. Would you like to sit over at Carews' this afternoon while I go downtown?"

"No, I'll stay here."

Bea never relaxed. Even at meals she was always thinking ahead to what she would do next, Marcia thought. She wondered if Bea ever really enjoyed anything.

Marcia folded her napkin and looked across the small cluttered kitchen while Orville finished. She felt stifled and she couldn't look at either of them. She sat with colorless, vacant eyes, troubled that she could have let herself come to such a pass. She wanted to get away by herself. Sometimes, at night, she dreamed she was running like a girl again up the quarry road, making the branches stir as she passed.

"I guess this kitchen must be hot; it makes you so drowsy, Mrs. Elder," Bea said.

Wednesday nights, when Bea went to prayer-meeting, Orville and Marcia sat quietly in the crowded parlor, Orville reading the paper, Marcia sitting idle, with her hands still.

"Want the radio, Mrs. Elder?"

"No, thank you, Orville."

Then they seldom spoke again until Bea came home.

Thursdays, Orville took Bea to the movies.

"I don't know's I ought to leave you in the house alone at night, Mrs. Elder . . ." Bea worried until the moment that they left, even stopping on the steps of the porch to call back to her, "You're sure you'll be all right? I left Hattie Carew's number marked out plain on the telephone book."

"Yes, I'll be all right. I'll sit right here till you come."

Then the silence of the small house closed around her as the stillness of the big house on the hill never had. She looked at the black filigree of the hot air register resentfully. She had been trapped into this house, this way of living, because it was easy to keep warm here. Fear of cold was an old woman's undoing. You could get by the fear of loneliness after a while. You could keep remembering back so you mixed the present with the past, and you could pretend that things had to be done so you kept busy but you couldn't keep warm by pretending. Sitting there in Bea's over-stuffed chair, as warm as she could ask to be—too warm, waves of hot dry heat came up out of the filigree register as though from a baking oven—Marcia faced her own weakness. Then, half guiltily, she went over to stand a minute on the register until the hot air rose under her skirts, clothing her limbs like warm flannel.

EIGHT

MARCIA was surprised at the darkness of the kitchen this morning. Bea must be up. Marcia had sat in her room until after she heard Orville shake the furnace. But the kitchen was empty. Marcia looked into the dining room, but that, too, was empty. Then Orville came up from the basement. He looked almost scared. He hadn't shaved this morning and Bea always insisted on that. Marcia had heard her scold about it.

"Bea's sick," Orville said.

The idea was strange. Bea seemed too strong for sickness ever to catch up with her.

Marcia frowned. "Real bad?"

Orville shook his head. "I don't know. She's got an awful pain in her arm. She says it's a heart attack. I wanted to get a doctor in the night but she wouldn't let me. She broke something under her nose and breathed it."

They were like two guilty children whispering together in the dark kitchen.

"I never knew she had a bad heart," Marcia said.

"I didn't either. She says she's always had it."

Marcia stood fingering her shawl, bewildered by the discovery of weakness in Bea. Then she looked at Orville. His shoulders drooped. His thin, unshaven face was woebegone.

"Well, I'll make some porridge and put the coffee on," she said.

Marcia was clumsy getting breakfast in the small kitchen. She let the porridge boil over and dropped a spoon on the floor. The clatter made her hand tremble for minutes afterwards. She set a tray for Bea and had to change the napkin on it because she dripped the coffee pouring it. When she had it ready she went timidly to Bea's door.

Bea lay with her eyes closed. Orville took the tray and set it on the dresser. Marcia went back to the kitchen.

Now the sun came in across the sink-board and shone across the blue and orange cupboards. When Bea had the light on, you never saw the sun come in. Morning sun was a holy thing. It came so softly; you ought to be waiting for it, not so impatient you had to flash on the hard, bright electric light. Then she felt guilty for her thought. Bea was sick.

Orville came across the passageway into the kitchen, tiptoeing ponderously. He had forgotten to slip his arms through his suspenders and looked like a horse out of harness. His shirt had little hollowed places on the shoulders where the suspenders usually rode. He sat down to breakfast and ate silently. He must care about Bea in his way, Marcia thought.

"Bea said to get Hattie Carew's biggest girl in to do for us until she gets up on her feet. I'll go over right after breakfast."

"I think I can manage," Marcia said stoutly.

Orville shook his head. "You know how Bea is; she wouldn't hear to it."

How strange it was, Marcia thought, to be eating breakfast here with Orville Greenstead. She could remember when he was a sheepish-looking boy on Sunday-school picnics. His mother had been a Springer girl, always a meek sort. She had never thought much of her. Life twisted things around so and made you come up at last with people you had spurned.

"More coffee, Orville?"

Orville shook his head sadly.

III

When Hattie Carew's oldest girl came over, Hattie came with her. She was like Bea.

"Now, Mrs. Elder, don't you worry one bit. You just sit here by the front window and watch the street while I look after Bea."

And Marcia sank down in the rocker obediently. Her knees were shaky. It was good to sit still.

Hattie sent for the doctor and when he came he and Orville stood out on the front porch in the cold November day and talked. Marcia looked past them down the street.

The day had turned gray after the first shy morning sun. Maple Street looked gloomy. There were not enough leaves left to scuffle through, no bright ones to press in books. The school children went straight along. Brown leaves must lie deep in the wagon ruts on Ryder hill now, wet and shiny like the backs of small brown snails. But the balsam and spruce trees saved November days from dullness up there, and the birch trees, pockmarked with brown eyes, like potatoes, always gleamed out white.

Marcia's face was like a child's as she sat with her hands in her lap. Her mouth smiled faintly. She could not have told what she was thinking, her thoughts ran so brokenly through her mind.

When Marcia opened her eyes and looked around the tight little parlor, Orville sat with his face in his hands. Hattie Carew came out of Bea's room with a shocked look on her face. Her oldest girl moved around the kitchen softly, looking in like a startled rabbit whenever she passed the doorway.

"Oh, Mrs. Elder, we didn't want to wake you." Hattie Carew came across and sat down by Marcia and took her hand. "It's been a terrible shock to all of us. I hate to break it to you, but . . . Bea . . . passed away."

The room was still. They sat like a prayer-meeting congregation waiting for the spirit to move. Marcia looked at each one, then at Bea's closed door. It was hard to believe. In a minute, Bea must come hurrying through that door and plump the sofa pillow into shape that Orville had shucked down behind him, and send all these people about their business.

"She had another attack and it took her off, just like that!" Hattie Carew said. "It's an awful shock for you at your age."

Marcia stood unsteadily, not sure just what she wanted to do, only feeling more equal to things on her feet. She took hold of the back of the chair and tried to realize that Bea had died.

"You've made arrangements?" she asked Hattie. The question was almost automatic, she had attended to the last rites for the dead so many times. "It's hard for Bea to die, just when she had her way," Marcia said slowly, more to herself than the others.

Hattie Carew looked startled that Mrs. Elder could talk like that. Orville stared at her.

"Well, Orville, she left you and me to comfort each other," Marcia added almost briskly.

"I declare," Hattie Carew said afterwards to the neighbors, "I didn't know that old lady could be so sprightly. It was almost as though she took ahold of things."

At the funeral, Marcia Elder sat in the chair beside Orville. Now and then, during the minister's words, a sigh that was like a sob ran through Orville and she glanced at him almost curiously. Marcia sat as she had at so many funerals, hearing the words that had taken on such a rightness of cadence that they had ceased to be ominous. They were as the shadow of the afternoon sun moving across the soapstone doorstep, the coming of dusk, the fading into night. About these others in the room there was a tenseness of bated breath, a superstitious dread of death that yet held them fascinated.

Orville Greenstead sat like a child who had been punished. He had been washed along into marriage by Bea's determination. She had pointed out that there would be cozy evenings, and the regular meals and a house kept by a woman would be a comfort. There needed to be no foolishness about it, Bea had said. And he had looked around his house that was forlorn enough, at his full mending basket, and the smoked chimney, and had agreed. But once he had gone to live with Bea, his whole soul had revolted at her bossing him. He had minded secretly when Bea smoothed his hair in front of Mrs. Elder. And now Bea had died. It was a judgment on him.

He glanced at Mrs. Elder and the calm of her small pale face, her mouth with the lips lying in a smooth line together, comforted him. He caught her glance and for all that her eyes had grown small between the wrinkled folds of flesh, they were clear and bright. They seemed to know his guilt and not make over-much of it. Orville sighed again, but he felt a little eased.

Marcia let the words run over her, like the water running over her fingers in the brook back of the house: ". . . we bring our years to an end, as a tale that is told. The days of our age are three score years and ten. . . ."

Only hers, Marcia Elder's, were four score and four. Why, no one knew. She didn't take unusual care of herself. She just kept well and lived on. She had looked on her life as all done when she let Bea have the auction. She had come down to Dedham because she couldn't last long and Bea was so set on it. Bea kept talking and she grew tired of holding out against her. Now Bea had died. She was free to do as she liked again; to have the potatoes baked instead of fried, to make the pie-crust her own way, to let the morning sun come into the room by itself. . . .

The minister was praying, saying the same words she had heard at Will's funeral and John's, "Oh, Lord Jesus Christ, who by thy death did'st take away the sting of death . . ."

"Mrs. Elder, do you think you better go out to the cemetery? Hadn't you better stay right here and lie down, it'll be a strain on you."

Marcia shook her head. "No, I'll go to keep Orville company."

They drove out in the Carews' car, she and Orville in the back seat, silent; Orville ashamed that he was not grieving more, Marcia lost in the thought of so many other funerals, both trying to make up by their presence for their lack of love for Bea.

The minister's words came to an end. There was that reluctant hush before the living turned back to living. They walked softly a few rods, then, at a decent distance, their feet hit the gravel naturally again. Marcia and Orville lingered a few minutes longer. Poor Bea, some of the auction money would go to pay for her funeral, Marcia thought with compassion. Then she and Orville followed the others back to the living.

NINE

D ON'T you want I should leave Sara here to do up the dishes after you're through, Mrs. Elder?" Hattie Carew asked.

"No, it'll be quieter for just the two of us. There won't be many dishes," Marcia said.

"Well, that's so, and it isn't as if Orville weren't handy, 'cept he's so shook up," she added in a whisper. "I tell you, you stood it real good." Then she went out, leaving some cold meat and a loaf of bread and a bowl of sauce on the table.

Orville still sat slumped in his chair, uncomfortable in his best black suit, the suit he had been married in.

He held his face in his hands and looked out the window without seeming to see anything. Marcia stood an instant looking at him. Orville Greenstead was a putterer way through, at working or living. Then she pulled the shade behind him and turned on the table lamp.

"I'll have supper ready in a minute, Orville," she said. Orville made her feel stronger, he looked so done in.

She was very slow around the kitchen. It tired her to have to think of everything at once. She forgot to warm the teapot and threw the tea out to do it. Waste didn't count tonight. It had been so long since she had had tea just right. She spread a clean cloth even though it was only Wednesday night.

They ate silently. Marcia forgot Orville. There was no need to hurry or talk. She could drink her tea as slowly as she pleased.

"Seems queer without Bea, don't it?" Orville asked. His face was blotched as though from crying, yet he hadn't been.

Marcia looked at him. Did he feel he ought to mourn Bea? Or had he really cared for her? She couldn't tell.

"Let me give you some more tea, Orville."

He pushed his cup over to her and she filled it. Bea's china teapot didn't pour like her old brown one. She wondered with a pang who had the brown teapot.

After the dishes Marcia went on into her room to bed.

She undressed slowly and lay down. Her whole body ached; the pain in her legs was worse. She closed her eyes in the dark but she couldn't sleep.

She tried to plan out how they would manage. She had lain this way at night in her bedroom up on the hill and planned out what was best to do a year ago. Now it was all to do over again. She would have to get someone in to do the hard work. Perhaps Orville would go back to Ryder village to live. He'd have to spunk up a little. She supposed he had a right to this house, though. She had, too.

She got out of bed to raise the window higher, and looked out across the Carews' backyard. The wind was coming up. It was blowing twice as hard as it had been at the cemetery. It flopped the Carews' clothes reel around and rattled the single Maple tree that stood between the houses. Then it died away in a rustle of old newspapers on the walk. There was no rising roar in it that came from a hundred trees on the hillside.

Marcia got back into bed and pushed the sheet down so she could lie next to the blanket. At home she could lie in bed and look out the window at the sky through the elm tree. She could hear the brook. It rested her to pretend that she was back again. It was never lonely there as it was in this small house of Bea's.

Almost as though she knew where her thoughts were

leading, she squeezed the blanket in her hands and lay very still in bed.

Why not? There was no one to stop her. She could make Orville drive her up there. There was snow in the air tonight but they could get through if they started early.

She wanted to hear the wind again sweeping down Ryder hill, blowing the water in the brook the wrong way, so it looked like a gray tiger cat with its hair ruffled. Mournful, Bea said the sound of the wind was, but not if you had been born to the sound of it, and run down the hill in the wind as a child, and gone away with your lover with the wind turning the leaves backward as you passed, and come back alone and cried yourself to sleep when the wind blew.

All night, she kept waking and remembering that to-morrow she was going back home.

She was up before Orville in the morning, moving around the kitchen making a lunch and breakfast at the same time. She waited until he came up from the basement to tell him.

"Orville, I want you to drive me back up Ryder hill, today. We'll start right after breakfast." Her voice had never grown feeble. Now it was clear and quiet, a little faster than usual.

"But, Mrs. Elder, that road . . . You can't tell anything about the weather this time of year. It'll be cold as a barn up there now. I couldn't think of taking you up there."

"Orville, I've made up my mind. If you're afraid to drive up there, I can likely hire someone."

While Orville was drinking his coffee and Marcia was buttering bread for sandwiches, the snow began. Marcia saw the flakes first, coming out of the early morning dark as softly as milkweed seeds. Orville was too busy eating to notice.

The flakes weren't piling up fast, only powdering the ground lightly, like sugar on a cruller, Marcia told herself. She wrapped her sandwiches in wax paper and packed them in a box. It made her think of box lunches she had packed years and years ago when Orville Greenstead was in short skirts.

Orville pushed back his chair. "Don't you want to smoke your pipe, Orville? My brothers used to smoke," she offered. Bea had only let him smoke outdoors.

A sheepish smile crept over Orville's face.

"I don't know's Bea'd like it here in her kitchen," he said, sobering.

"I don't believe they're bothered with small matters in Heaven, Orville."

But as he went over to the stove to get a match, he saw the snow.

"Look there, Mrs. Elder!"

"I know, but it won't amount to much. We're going anyway, Orville." Marcia's face was set. Nothing would stop her today. She wanted to see winter come once more on the hill. She would have seen eighty-three winters come up there; only one she had been in Illinois. She felt a little giddy at her sudden strength.

She rinsed the dishes and let them stand. She put on her warmest clothes and got out her minkskin coat that was twenty-two years old, and a black knit hood.

"Better dress warm, Orville!" she warned.

Orville sat uncomfortably reading the morning paper. He was going to try to hold out against her.

She came out now all ready, with a hot water bottle and extra mittens and blankets. She knew she had tried to do too much, her head ached and she felt dizzy.

Orville looked at her. "It would be wrong, Mrs. Elder, to take you off up . . ."

"Orville, if you're scared to drive the car up Ryder hill, say so, and I'll get someone else." She felt as though she were daring one of her brothers.

Orville shifted his eyes and frowned as he studied the snow. He shook his head slowly. Marcia never took her gaze from him. Her coat was too warm in the house, but she wouldn't unbutton even the neck of it. The tight little parlor was painfully still. Then Orville got up and went into his bedroom.

"I suppose we could drive over as far as Ryder village, but even that's fool-hardy with it starting to snow," he temporized.

Marcia's face relaxed. She put the lunch-box on top of the blankets.

TEN

THEY drove without talking. The snow-flakes came against the windshield so fast they blocked the wiper. When the car slowed the wiper rubbed faster across the glass and left a clear view of the snowy road. But on Marcia's side the windshield was an even pane of frosted glass. She held her mittened hands clasped tight together inside her large, old-fashioned muff. It didn't matter that she could see nothing ahead but a snowy glass darkened by moving tips of trees; she was going back home.

"If we can make the hill, which I don't think we can, you're liable to get your death a-cold traipsing around that old house."

Marcia laughed and hugged her muff to her. "You sound just like Bea, Orville!"

Orville looked at Mrs. Elder sideways. She acted queer.

"What would Bea think?" he brought out reprovingly, taking refuge in the thought of Bea's unfailing practicality.

Marcia laughed again. "It would kill her right off, Orville."

Her water bottle was cooling even under her coat. She could feel the cold up her legs in spite of the long tights she wore. She would be crippled up with rheumatism for a week and the neuralgia in her shoulder would be worse, but wild horses couldn't drag a murmur out of her. This was the first time since Bea had come to live with her that she had felt free. It went to her head more than a whole glass of blackberry cordial.

"I believe we went off and left a bottle of cordial in the cellar-way. I forgot to tell Bea about it that day we left," she told Orville. "That will warm us up when we get there."

"I never take spirits," Orville said virtuously.

"Nothing like it to warm you up and keep off a chill, Orville; nothing better for summer complaint, either."

"We'll stop at the store and ask about the road," Orville said as they drove into Ryder. "And if no one's been up over it this week, we'll turn around. You can see the snow's getting deeper all the time." It was a long speech for Orville. He brought it out in jerks.

He stopped the car in front of the store and pulled his squirrel-skin cap farther down over his head, turning the collar of his coat up to meet it. The narrow V of face that showed between looked sharp, not like that of a man who could be badgered by women.

"I'll go in and warm up," Marcia said. The snow had piled at the edge of the path so Orville picked Mrs. Elder up and lifted her over it. They were both surprised.

"Why, Orville, you're a regular gallant!"

Against his will, Orville smiled. Then he kicked at the snow in the walk and brought himself back to the knowledge that Mrs. Elder was eighty-four and that Bea, his wife, died three days ago.

The store was half dark because of the winter day and the pyramids of canned tomatoes and peas that blocked the two front windows.

"How do you do, Asa," Marcia said to the gray-haired man with the apron tied around his waist. She had taught Asa Houghton how to spell his own name.

"Why, Mrs. Elder, back in these parts on a day like this!" But his surprise was only mild. Then he remembered something. The memory brought his head forward a little. He straightened his glasses. "Amy heard that Mrs. Cannon died?" He asked it in a hoarse whisper out of deference to Orville who stood up in front selecting a can of tobacco.

"That's right; heart attack," Marcia answered. "Asa, when Orville asks you how the Ryder hill road is I want you to tell him it's first rate." She held him by the edge of the bib of his apron. "Don't forget, Asa!"

Asa Houghton rubbed his head thoughtfully. Mrs. Elder made him feel like a little tike again.

"I don't believe there's been anybody down or up since you came down last August. When the snow gets good there'll be logging."

"Of course, there's been folks up the hill since last August. But never mind, I'm going up there today; Orville's going to drive me. Could you get this water bottle filled for me over at the house while I warm up? I want it good and hot, Asa!"

Asa took the water bottle from her like a boy filling the drinking dipper in school.

Marcia went back toward the modern stove that Asa had put in that fall: a mahogany-colored affair made to imitate a victrola. A tall slender woman in ski pants and fur jacket sat there with her feet against the stove. She was smoking a cigarette. At Marcia's "how do you do," she nodded.

"How do you do."

Marcia went straight to the business of getting warm and, while the men were at a safe distance, turned her skirts up to her knees so she could feel the direct heat on her legs that looked thinner in their black tights.

"I imagine they're warmer than skirts," Marcia said to the stranger, nodding at her pants.

The young woman laughed. "They don't let the snow up and they're water-proof. They're the only thing for skiing."

Marcia considered that. It was a new word to her.

The young woman made a sliding motion with her hands. "Like they do in the Alps, you know," she explained.

"Have you been doing that up here?" Marcia turned her back to the stove.

"The snow's no good yet, but I didn't really come to ski," she said.

A little silence fell between them, a well-bred Vermonter's silence, in which Marcia speculated on the purpose of this stranger's visit. It had the usual result. The young woman seemed to feel that further explanation was needed.

"I'm thinking of starting it up here, if I can find a place. The storekeeper tells me nobody has the time for such foolishness." Her smile suggested that Marcia would enjoy the remark, too. "But there are plenty of people who do have who would love it up here."

"You mean a place where people from the city could come?" Marcia asked slowly.

The young woman nodded. "Small groups. Most places are too big. This would have to be very special."

Marcia had dropped her skirts. Her hands were clasped tightly together inside her muff. She had forgotten the pain in her legs.

"If you could find an old farmhouse, that might do," she suggested in a quiet voice.

"Yes, but I've asked the storekeeper. He's very discouraging."

"I suppose it ought to be up on one of these hills." She made it a statement rather than a question.

"Yes, with a view. Of course, it couldn't be too far away or too inaccessible."

Asa came back into the store with the hot water bottle, but Marcia sat down in a chair and pulled it closer to the stove.

"They built those old hill roads to last," she said. "Of course, they're grown over and some of them need a little widening, but they'll take you there. You have to climb a hill if you're going to get any kind of view."

"Yes," the young woman agreed, lighting a fresh cigarette. "But they tell me most of the hill farms have been deserted so long they've gone to rack and ruin."

"Most of them have," Marcia said. She put her mittened hand to her mouth a second, uncertain, then she said softly, "I know of a brick one that's as sound as the year it was built. It's been lived in since 1802. That's what keeps a house alive." She was breathing a little hard so she had to stop a minute.

"This one has a big open attic and four big bedrooms on the second floor, one down . . . twice as big as the bedrooms they have in bungalows. You could cut them in two and still have something. There's a parlor, a sitting room, dining room, kitchen . . ." She counted them on her fingers. "A spring runs right into the house; you never tasted such water . . ."

"Sounds good, but there must be a catch somewhere; there always is," the young woman said.

Marcia stood up and let the heat strike directly on the shoulder that would have neuralgia tonight. Her light blue eyes that were half hidden by their wrinkled lids sharpened. When she spoke again, her voice shook ever so little.

"It's only three miles out from the village and it's for sale, all but the southwest corner. That's made into a separate apartment for the owner."

"How strange; why that, do you suppose?"

"It's in the first deed back in 1816, and the owner likes living there."

The tall young woman stamped out her cigarette and took out a pad from one of her pockets.

"It'll probably be a false hope like all the rest of my leads, but I'd like to look it over. I don't suppose I better try to see it until this storm is over."

135

"I'm going there right now," Marcia said firmly. "It's my place."

"I began to wonder if it weren't," the young woman said with a smile. "How much are you asking for it?"

"I'll think that out on the way up." Marcia walked to the front of the store, not letting herself look back to see if the young woman followed.

"Thank you, Asa." She took the hot water bottle from him. "Well, we'll go along. I'm glad the road's so good. Orville, did you hear what Asa said about the road?"

Asa looked at Marcia. Then he nodded his head.

"It's . . . I ain't heard nothing bad about it yet."

The young woman came up beside her. "This is Orville Greenstead; he's going to drive us up the hill," Marcia said, briskly turning to her. "What was your name?"

"Claire Stellwagon."

"Mine's Marcia Elder. Well, we can go, then."

Asa Houghton stood back of the pyramid of cans in the front window and watched them go. It was just as Amy said, Mrs. Elder was so old she was probably a little queer in the head, but Orville Greenstead ought to know better than to be led on by her. Funny now that he hadn't thought to tell that city woman about the Wyman place when she was asking, but being up on that hill, it clean slipped his mind.

"If it looks bad we'll turn back at the covered bridge," Orville croaked ominously.

"It's never bad there," Marcia answered. She was waiting to hear the rattle of the loose planks of the covered bridge again. She could remember the bridge being built when she was a child.

"You want to get a good start for the hill, Orville," Marcia warned. "Maybe you better put your chains on now." She was a general directing a campaign.

Orville got out grumpily and put on the chains. In the interval, Claire Stellwagon tried to find out more about the house.

"I've been away for a short time," Marcia told her. "I made a mistake ever leaving."

The snow falling steadily closed in any view. The car breathed a cloud of steam from its radiator; the windshield wiper stopped altogether. The three occupants of the car were silent, tense, leaning a little forward in a concerted effort to help it up the road.

"There ain't a sign of a track in the road," Orville muttered.

"Of course not, with this fresh snow," Marcia answered cheerfully.

Just where a Maple tree hung out over the road like a black finger of warning, the car seemed to slide backward; at least, it gained no ground. Orville was frightened. He grabbed for the emergency brake and the car spun around in the road as smoothly as a paper on a pin.

"Drive it to the inside, Orville!" Marcia said. In her excitement her voice cracked.

But Orville had frozen to the wheel. Claire Stellwagon reached across Marcia and turned it so that the car careened toward the woods at one side, up against the bank, and came to a stop.

"Mrs. Elder, do you want all of us to be killed?" Orville implored in a shaken voice.

Claire Stellwagon laughed aloud. She was leaning over in front of Orville, half crushing the little old woman between them.

"Orville, we won't be killed. Get out and find a log to put under the wheels. You better drive," Marcia said to Claire.

"But the whole thing's a fool business. We can't climb that hill. Look at the snow!" Orville protested.

"I see it. Orville, you get busy and find some logs."

Orville got out of the car as though he were afraid it would tip over. He had to stoop to look in the window at the two women and the snow coming down in big flakes fell on his nose and lips and caught in the bristles of his beard.

"Hurry, Orville. We can't stay here till dark!" Marcia called, rolling down the window. Orville peered in and his eyes showed genuine fright.

"Mrs. Elder, I'm not going a step farther."

"All right, Orville; put the logs under the wheels and walk back to town. We'll manage." Marcia's voice was shrill with daring. So she had shamed Matt into riding a sled down this same hill, standing up, more than seventy years ago. Being back on this hill did something to her. Her feeble old legs felt strong.

"You get in back of the wheel and we'll put Orville in the back seat," Marcia told Claire Stellwagon. "He's too scared to drive, but we'll need him up at the house."

When the logs were under the wheels Orville got in. Claire started the car, letting it roar a little. Marcia leaned over and wiped the windshield with her muff.

The car hesitated, lurched forward, then stalled. Orville mumbled in the back seat.

"Would it do any good if Orville pushed?" Marcia asked.

Claire shook her head. "We can make it, if the snow doesn't get any deeper."

She started the car again. This time it climbed, as though defying snow and gravity and the whole desolate hillside.

"Keep going now!" Marcia cried above the roar, leaning over to dab at the windshield again. "We'll make it! We'll be there for the first snowstorm of the year! We'll make smoke come out of the chimney and the lights shine across the brook!" She half sang her phrases to a triumphant tune of her own chanting. "I never should have left it, never! I should have died up here where I was born. There's the opening to the quarry road, remember, Orville! You can't see . . ." Her voice trailed off into silence as she strained her eyes against the snow-covered windshield.

The snow was deeper as the road climbed between the tall timber of her woodlot on one side and the stone wall on the other. It was only a little after midday but the sky had darkened as though it had lost track of time and were already slipping into dusk.

"This is pretty far from town," Claire ventured once.

"Not really," Marcia answered quickly. "It's only the snow and Orville's taking on that make it seem so. When you come around the next curve you turn in between two posts." Marcia's voice was hushed. Claire shifted back from second into low, ready for the turn.

"There!" Marcia whispered before Claire could see anything but trees and falling snow. "Back against the hill!" Marcia pointed, and Claire made out the gable of the tall brick house.

There were the two granite posts, topped with snow, but the snow had made the driveway level with the rest of the ground.

"You'll have to stop the car here and walk up the

path," Marcia said in a thin, excited voice. Somehow, she managed to be ahead of them and pull open the picket gate wide enough to slip through. Claire hurried after her and tried to take her arm but Marcia needed no help.

The bare branches of the trees stood gibbet-like against the snow. But the faded red bricks of the house seemed to give out a reassuring warmth, and framed the two doors, one wide and one narrow, each topped by its fan window.

Marcia produced the big iron key from her muff. "Bea had it hidden in the flour bin, back of the sacks," she told Claire cryptically and Orville shuffled his feet a little. She swung back the door and the sharper cold of empty rooms rushed out at them.

"Orville, you see if you can build fires in both stoves. There's still plenty of wood in the shed, and bring some boxes to sit on," Marcia said briskly.

Claire followed her out to the kitchen that was bare except for the big range.

"Best water in the township flows in here," Marcia said, touching the soapstone cistern. She went to the cellar door and disappeared down in the clammy dark, coming back up with a long-necked bottle covered with dust. "I put this cordial up in 1925," she read from the faded label. "I guess there aren't any glasses left so we'll have to drink from the bottle. It'll warm us till the fires are going." She passed it to Claire and then took a swallow herself. The cordial spread burning warmth through her body.

"Now you can see the rest of the house!" Marcia led the way through room after room, each dark in the winter day and yet not dreary because their deep-set small-paned windows looked on so much of the snowy world.

Marcia sat by the kitchen stove while Claire made a tour of the second floor. When she came back, Marcia said abruptly, "You can have this place as it stands for whatever you think is right, if you'll keep it up and let me live in the southwest corner. Anybody who would drive the hill road today would be fit to have it. Come along and I'll show you where I would live, just as I was meant to."

Claire followed her out of the front door into the snow, past the parlor windows to the narrow second door. The room inside was stripped of all furniture but a parlor stove and the empty book shelves. Behind the front room was a small kitchen and, off to the side, a bedroom.

"It gets the southern sun that's kindest to old people." Marcia stood so long in the front room, looking out through the window, that Claire touched her arm.

"Are you all right?"

Marcia turned toward her. All the exhilaration of the ride had run out of her. Her face was gray and pinched. The pale blue eyes were the dead gray color of the snowy sky.

"I'm tired," she said. "We can't go back tonight. Orville will have to fix up beds of boughs around the stove. I put some blankets in the car and there's some food . . ."

After they were warmed by the fire and had eaten, Marcia left Claire helping Orville with the beds and went out to stand on the doorstep. It was dark now; only the falling snow-flakes seemed to have a light and sound of their own. Her shoulder ached and her legs were lame, but she had to step out into the snow. She held out her hands and felt the gentle flakes. The wet snow came above her overshoes but she didn't care.

"Now," she whispered. It would be nice to die now. There couldn't be any more excitement in life after this. She had been here again for the first snowstorm and now she was tired, through and through.

But a wind from the hill stirred the branches of the elm tree, a cold wind that blew the smell of pines to her. Marcia breathed it in eagerly. A dark shadow broke away from the trees, two points of fire flashed toward her. Against the white, unbroken field of snow that

stretched to the hill, she saw a body arch itself and dis-
appear again into the darker shadows.

Like a child, Marcia hurried back to the house.

"I saw a deer," she said. "As close to the house as that
row of currant bushes!"

CPSIA information can be obtained at www.ICGtesting.com
Printed in the USA
BVOW05s1512191014

371310BV00001B/7/P